Harmony

Falls

Harmony Falls

A Fresh Start

By Marii Larsen

Harmony Falls
By Marii Larsen
Copyright © 2013

TMN/Wisdom Merchants
P.O. Box 481
Klamath Falls, Oregon 97601
First Edition 2013

ISBN 13: 978-0-9894735-1-4
ISBN 10: 0989473511

Scars, whether physical or emotional,
remind us where we've been,
They do not dictate where we're going
Scars are not our final destination!

Author
Unknown

Reviews

An excellent book to read! Very engaging, something new and exciting with every page turned. I would recommend this book to anyone!

-Vicki T.
Homemaker

WOW! A must read! I couldn't put the book down! Not only was it entertaining to read but has a powerful message as well!

Anna C.
Retired R.N.

HARMONY FALLS, A Fresh Start written by Marii Larsen is a refreshing look into the resilience of soul and determination of mind. The factional book is a look into the lives of a number of women who have experienced abusive relationships and lived to tell about is as well as to be renewed and refreshed. Their experiences have been artfully woven into the character of Sandi Johnson. "Her" story is sadly one to which many in our society can relate. I consider this book and the following volumes to be must read for anyone involved in an abusive relationship.

Velma Crow
Minister, Author, Artist

Dedication

This book is dedicated to my wonderful and loving parents, who encouraged me daily, and to my faithful friend and soul mate Norman Larsen. Special thanks to my writing mentor Velma Crow who has given invaluable wisdom and advise throughout, and helped bring this book into being, to my writer's guild members Kathy Wilson and Penny Hansen, who wouldn't let me quit, but kept asking what will happen next. In addition I want to thank my children, Melanie Kunau, Juree Raugutt and her husband Nate, and Renee Hart and her husband Nick, whose enthusiasm was inspiring, and many others who would not let me give up. Thank you to my friend, neighbor and walking partner friend, Vicki, who gave me fresh insight daily. Thank you to all who had a part in making this work of fiction a reality.

Chapter 1

Officer Mike Bradford pulled up behind the rusted Ford pickup. The deserted stretch of River Road had occasional traffic as it wound thru the thick woods, toward Beaver dam. Known for great hunting and fishing, there were no homes in this area, so finding a parked truck in the middle in winter was an ominous sign, especially one covered in snow. Mike wondered how long it had been here, he really did not want to get out of the warm patrol car to check the vehicle, but duty calls. A blast of icy cold wind hit him, sending chills down his spine as he stepped out of his K-9 cruiser. Rex, his canine partner, jumped out pushing past him, raced toward the dam, barking.

"Rex," He whistled. "Here boy."

"Nothing on those plates." cracked the radio.

"10-4" replied Mike as he wrapped his coat tighter against the biting cold winter wind.

Walking up to the truck, Bradford shined his flashlight into the bed of the truck…nothing. Looking inside, there wasn't much, just a light coat, and a flashlight on the seat. The rifle rack on the back window was bare, except for a lone fishing pole. *This guy sure wasn't prepared for the winter.*

Mike did not want to search for anyone in the deep snow especially in this steep terrain, but the urgent barking of the police dog sounded as if he had found something. Grumbling about the bitter cold, Bradford whistled for the dog. A stocky man in his early thirties, he felt trekking thru the woods at his age was, well it was for younger, much younger officers; *A nice warm desk job sounded real nice right now, in fact it sounded down right cozy, but he knew he wouldn't be happy sitting at a desk all day, pushing paper.* No, Mike loved his job; he could do without the bitter winters of Harmony Falls, and the deep snowfalls.

Shaking the snow off his boots, he walked back to his cruiser, and notified dispatch. Grabbing his rifle, and a heavier coat, Mike began to carefully pick his way along the steep embankment, toward the dam. A split second later, the snowy edge of the embankment gave way as Bradford slipped and lost his footing. Sliding downward out of control toward the river, Mike held desperately onto his rifle. Unbearable pain shot through his ankle as it twisted in an effort to stop his mad decent. The cold snow bit into his face, feeling like a thousand shards of glass tearing into his flesh as he spiraled down, out of control. Unable to get his bearings, in the swirling blind plunge, Bradford grabbed at blackberry bushes with his free hand, the sharp thorns of the branches tore at his hands, and face before he was finally jerked to a stop at the water's edge near the base of the dam, jamming his injured foot against the unforgiving rocks. Nearly passing out from the blinding pain, He stared at the water's edge as it slowly came into focus, his foot askew in an odd position. He sat there stunned as a cloud of disturbed snow settled around him, showering him with a mantle of icy crystals. Slowly the realization of what had just happened broke thru the blurred fog of snow, pain, ice and thorns, as if he had participated in a theatrical production. The agony of the biting cold and his twisted ankle jerked him out of his trance. Taking a deep breath, trying to ease the intense pain, then slowly comprehended his predicament.

Looking around to gather his bearings, Mike stared straight in to the face of a man! His heart jumped! "Ayah" Bradford yelled unnerved by the unexpected encounter, almost passing out from the blinding pain in his ankle, as he scrambled backward. The man didn't move. Heart pounding, Mike calmed himself, then leaned forward, and took a closer look at the man. The man stared… frozen in time. He wasn't anyone the officer had seen around before.

"Buddy, are you alright?" Mike asked as he reached over to shake him.

The man toppled stiffly over; the frosty pallor of his face frozen in the realization of impending doom.

Bradford then noticed dried blood that stained the front of the man's parka and surrounding snow, appearing to have come from a gunshot wound to his chest. Dressed in hunting attire, the man's hat had been pulled down over his ears. Icicles hung off his hair and the edges of his hat, his arms crossed in an effort to try to ward off the frigid overnight temperatures. Covered in a blanket of snow, the man had been huddled up against the structure of the dam, as he tried to seek shelter for last night's storm.

The officer, looked around the area for a weapon, but did not find one.

Sharp pain reminded Bradford of his sprained ankle; He loosened his boot and pealed back his sox. His ankle was not just sprained but broken; the bone protruding slightly under the skin, his ankle was already swollen twice its normal size, had turned a vivid purple color. Climbing uphill on his broken ankle would be out to the question, especially on the treacherous snowy incline; Mike tried to contact dispatch on the portable radio mounted on his shoulder......nothing......He tried again......nothing. The signal must be blocked, by the structure of the dam. Hearing something rustling in the berry bushes behind him, Bradford grabbed his rifle, wincing against the pain, rolled on his side, looking down the sight and aimed; waiting... for whomever or whatever to emerge from the underbrush. Heart pounding, he prayed it would not be a bear, coming down to fish the river, or worse yet, someone coming back to make sure the hunter had been finished off! Rex, his canine partner emerged, from the brambles. "I'm so glad it's you." Mike sighed in relief as he took comfort in the dog's presence.

The officer tried his radio again, there was still no response. Taking it off his shoulder clip, to check it out, he quickly discovered the radio cord had been severed during his fall. *Well, this has been a mighty fine afternoon, there is a reason I really don't like the winter storms here!* Mike thought sarcastically.

Tying the radio onto the dog's collar, he sent the dog back to town "Rex, Go get help, Go get Matt"

Matt was not only a fellow officer, but his twin brother as well, although they didn't look that much alike. Mike had sandy blonde hair while his older brother by all of two minutes had jet black hair and was three inches taller. They both were fortunate to serve the town of Harmony Falls together.

Watching Rex disappear over the top of the embankment Mike rubbed his hands together to keep them warm, then gathered kindling within reach. He built a small fire nestled against a large boulder, using his cigarette lighter. With the wall of the dam shielding him from some of the winter's bone-chilling wind and the warmth of the fire, Bradford tried to get comfortable as he warmed his hands over the fire, enjoying the warmth it provided.

....

Matt stepped out of the shower to answer the insistent phone. Whoever it is, really wanted to talk to him.

Picking up the receiver, Matt instantly regretted answering the call as he listened to Wilber Hawkins complain "Matt, Your blasted dog has been barking the last ten minutes." His neighbor was as cranky as they came. "Make him stop or I'll call the authorities"

I am the authorities Matt thought, checking beside his bed, he saw Max laying there watching him. "I'm sorry Mr. Hawkins, but it's not Max, he's sitting here inside my apartment. But I do hear a dog barking, I'll check it out."

Throwing on his bathrobe and slippers, Matt opened the sliding glass door, crossed his patio, shivering in the cold, and opened the back gate. Rex was outside the fencing barking. *Where's Mike?* Looking up and down the sidewalk, Matt didn't see Mike anywhere and felt instant foreboding "Rex, Hi boy, where's Mike? Come here Rex, Come on" *Mike is never without his canine, especially while on duty!*

"Come here Rex" He whistled. The canine turned and raced down the sidewalk, paused at the corner, waiting for Matt to follow him. Matt ran back inside and dressed quickly. Dread filling every fiber of his being as he feared for his brother's safety, he followed Mike's canine, out of town.

....

Mike turned to his cold companion searching the deceased's pockets. Locating his wallet, he scanned the driver's license "So your name in Raymond Wills. What were you doing up here? Why would anyone want to kill you? You have money in your wallet—so… it's not robbery. And you still have your coat and hat so they weren't after your warm clothes. The only injury seems to be the gunshot wound to your chest. You were a hunter, but the weapon is missing. Is that what they wanted? …Your gun? Sort of looks like a mafia hit, secluded, make sure there are no witnesses, and one shot to the chest to make sure you're gone." Writing down his observation, in his notepad Mike threw more kindling on the fire, again he tried to get more comfortable, as the vicious throbbing in his leg commanded his attention once again. He wondered if maybe he should put snow on the broken ankle, to slow the swelling, then deciding against it. Scanning the landscape Mike searched the area to make sure no one was returning to finish off the hunter.

Rustling in the bushes across the stream, produced a young deer, Mike watched as it started to nibble on the underbrush. *I wonder how they find enough food to survive on, especially with snow so deep, it covers absolutely everything, must be a sense of smell. How could sticks and twigs possibly smell good or even taste good? If it were me, I think I would starve on that diet!*

Observing the young deer forage on the forest floor, Mike relaxed a little, knowing if a predator was around the deer would bolt into the cover of the forest. A light snow began, each flake gracefully making its own way to earth, adding to the quiet and peaceful landscape. Beautiful crystal snowflakes hung in sparkling forms on nearby shrubs in sharp contrast to bright red rose hips of the wild rose bushes. Blackberry bushes bare of foliage formed interesting architectural arches as they lay in tangled snowy masses. Mike could barely tell where he had descended thru the brambles just a few minutes earlier. Thorny bushes encroaching on the base of the dam threatened to overtake the concrete fortress, in a constant struggle between man and nature. The towering wall of the dam stood in stark, rigid contrast to the graceful fluid lines of nature. Rocks layered under a blanket of snow lay in shapeless lumps lining the river, just inches from where he sat. Aspen trees, stately and bare, towering above him were in contrast to the dark green needles of the Douglas fir and Noble pines. A loud crack resounding throughout the forest announced a tree branch breaking under the weight of the snow.

Above him, in the lake side of the dam, you could catch the best rainbow, mackinaw, and catfish. There were some prize fish swimming up there. Landing one could give a fisherman the thrill of a lifetime. A small rivulet that poured from the restraints of the dam's spillway gurgled under a thin layer of ice, as it snaked its way out of sight. Bears loved to come down, fish the lake, and snack on the wild berries. Hunting dogs were a real asset in these woods above the quiet sleepy town. Bear attacks, although uncommon, had been known to happen.

…………

Matt followed as Mike's canine led him out of town and into the forest lands. It was hard to see the big German Shepherd through the heavily falling snow; the visibility was limited; at times Matt was unable to see the dog. Nearing the dam, Matt sighed in relief as he recognized his brother's patrol car up ahead. Already partially covered with snow it looked like a large lump. Calling into dispatch, Matt advised them of the location, as he watched Rex disappear thru the underbrush and down the embankment. Getting out of his squad car, he pulled his coat tighter as he stepped out into the falling snow, scanning the area he searched for clues as to what could have happened to his brother.

....

Mike and Matt had grown up in Harmony Falls, attended college in the big city and both returned home to serve on the police force. Mike had married his college sweetheart, Cindy. But Matt just hadn't "found the right one" as he would put it. The brothers had grown closer ever since their folks had been killed in an auto accident.

Mike was starting to get sleepy; he vigorously rubbed his arms on his chest and thighs in an effort to get his blood circulating. "Rub your body and the arms will take care of themselves" One of the first lessons you learned in survival training. The snow began to fall heavier as dusk approached, in an endless mesmerizing cascade of lacy white crystals, decorating the forest with a blanket of deceptive softness.

Silence is golden Mike thought *but not in this case, silence is a little unnerving, especially with my leg throbbing!*

Straining to listen in the deep silent snow he thought he heard someone calling *I'm losing it* He thought *Sure could use a strong cup of hot coffee to warm me right now.*

Throwing the last of kindling within reach onto the fire, the minutes dragged by Mike drowsily watched a six-point buck cautiously come down to the water's edge and drink, keeping a careful eye on the injured officer. Overhead a few little snow sparrows chattered among themselves scattered as Rex returned, and sat next to him.

…………

"Mike, Are you down there?" Matt carefully listening in the falling snow could barely make out the muffled reply "Yeah down here, I'm hurt, can't walk. And there is a body down here. Bring a bag."

"We'll have you up here soon. Rescue is on their way here. Just hang on" Matt called down. Within minutes the thump, thump, thump of the helicopter blades could be heard echoing off the wall of the dam. "Murder here? In Harmony Falls?" Officer Matt Bradford muttered to himself." Unheard of!"

Chapter 2

The petite blonde stood in front of the old farmhouse, squinting her green eyes, envisioning it with a fresh coat of paint and green...no blue...dark blue shutters. The wraparound porch would have hanging baskets of petunias and a cat cured up in a rocker, sleepily watching guests. The two story house would be perfect for her, although it was a bit big. There was a barn and beyond that was an orchard. The trees looked like apple and maybe a few pears, judging by the bark, they hadn't been trimmed in a few years from the looks of them. The barn seemed to be in good shape although in the snow she really couldn't tell, but it could house several horses. Just to the west of the property was forest land and a dam, that captured water, reclaiming it for irrigation of local farms.

Hearing a car pull up behind her, she turned to see a tall police officer get out "Can I help you?"

He asked. *I am so tired after staying up all night to recue Mike last night. I sure don't need to rescue some tourist out looking at property, especially if that old barn caves in because of the snow load. It was unusual to see someone looking at a house in this deep snow.*

Great the town cop, she thought. "No" Sandi replied loudly, maybe too loudly "I was just noticing the house was for sale and I might be interested" Inwardly she thought, *Go away and just let me think.*

"That house hasn't been lived in for near five years, Ever since old Mr. Ferguson passed away. Take a mite of work to turn it into a comfortable home." Matt Bradford continued.

That was obvious, she thought sarcastically as she nodded in agreement. *Please leave me alone so I can think!*

"Thinking of buying the place?" Bradford questioned her further as he sized her up. He had developed a keen eye and a quick judge of character since he had joined the force eleven years ago. *Her clothing suggests city life, She sure is a little jumpy, suppose that might come from city living too.*

"I might be, I suppose that would depend upon how much they want for the place"

In her native San Francisco, she couldn't have even hoped to purchase a home the real estate was just too expensive. But possibly, maybe she could afford one here. Turning she shrugged her shoulders, and struggled to walk back to her car in the deep snow.

Matt wondering about her abruptness followed her and held open the car door. "Hope to see you around then, Harmony Falls sure has been attracting a lot of new folks these days and it would be nice to see the old place lived in again." *Kind of a pretty little thing,* He thought.

"Well, thank you for your time, Officer." She snapped, Sandi could feel her defenses going up. Noticing how nice he looked in his uniform, she was determined not to be in another relationship.

"No problem. I'm Officer Matt Bradford; you can call me Matt, though."

"I'm Sandi Johnson." She replied.

"I'll see you around, Sandi." He answered smiling.

Getting in her car slowly she drove down the driveway almost getting stuck in the deep snow as she turned onto Main street.

That house would be almost perfect for me! She thought as she drove *the house itself is large for just one person, but the out building are great!* She had peeked in the kitchen window, and noticed the large stove and prep area, a big double sink near the kitchen window and another sink at the opposite end of the room, near a mud-room. The trees would be a real asset, it they could be trimmed. Sandi had always enjoyed growing her own food and canning it. *The large kitchen would be perfect for canning. Maybe Tammy would like to can, also, I wonder if she knows any good recipes!*

Sandi loved the small town feel of Harmony Falls. The slow-paced, old-fashioned life cherished by the residents, was just what she was looking for after moving out of the Bay area. *The driveway would have to be the first thing to be fixed though,* she thought as she pondered purchasing the house. Glancing in her rear view mirror, she could see the police cruiser still following behind her.

Great! She thought, *I move from a big city to a small town and the village cop has nothing better to do than to follow around prospective home buyers. Well, I guess I should have realized the crime rate here isn't as bad as back home. That's one thing I'll have to get used to. Who would have thought peace and quiet would be so...so...so challenging!*

In San Francisco crime was rampant and the deafening noise was constant, but here in this small town, it is quiet, everyone seemed relaxed, almost unaware of crime, most didn't see the need to lock their door. In this community, valued for its close-knit atmosphere, neighbors looked out for each other, everyone knew everyone, like a big family. Not like San Francisco where you could easily get lost in the big crowds.

When her sister, Tammy, had mentioned that the town's veterinarian was retiring in a year, Sandi jumped at the opportunity to live in Harmony Falls. It seemed like a dream come true. Tammy and her husband Bill talked often about how happy they were living in this tight knit community. Sandi welcomed the change. After her last mishap of a relationship the move seemed like a blessing from heaven. She thought back to that time, *He had seemed like such a thoughtful person in the beginning, but over time I noticed how possessive he became, how cruel. Then he started demanding that I quit my job to do his constant bidding, I thought we could work it all out, but then the violence. I was the one who had a job, he didn't. Oh sure, he bragged about his wonderful position at the construction company, until I found out later that he wasn't employed there-never had been employed there, in fact he spent his days at a bar. Wow, what a fight we had over that little lie! One time he had even taken the alternator out of my car which caused me to miss work. He just expected me to give up my dreams and a fulfilling career to stay home to wait on him, as he watched T.V. all day. Then when he had hit me...and the knife... that was it! No, No more relationships for me! This quiet community is just what I need after...... him. All I wanted was a peaceful home life, a shelter from the world, not a sparring match arena. Was that too much to ask*

Chapter 3

Driving to work the next morning, Sandi was deep in thought contemplating the house she had walked around yesterday, almost passing up her favorite shop.

Ahh Starbucks! She thought as she pulled in quickly *A little slice of heaven!*

Glancing in her rear view mirror, a police car pulled in right after her. *Great! How fast was I going? I know I was preoccupied. Speeds okay... ...well, just a little fast...maybe he is just getting coffee too.*

As the blue Chevy in front of her drove off. Sandi pulled up to the service window. In her mirror, she watched the cruiser pull up too and wait his turn.

"What will it be, Miss?"

"Yes, I think, I'll have a tall ……a tall………Yes, a tall vanilla latte"

"That will be $4.50," stated the young man as he handed her the most decadent latte she had ever tasted. Oh was it good! And the warmth was just as delicious that cold December morning. The good folks who worked for Starbucks are culinary geniuses!

Driving towards the veterinary clinic, she could see all the decorations going up, as the town was getting ready for the holidays. Snowflake banners hung from the downtown light poles, the church had a nativity scene on their front lawn, and many of the stores had set up displays hoping to entice shippers inside. The holiday spirit was everywhere, right down to the snow on the ground. The clinic had red and white twinkling lights illuminating the entrance. Sandi parked in her assigned space, and got out.

"Morning Sandi." a deep voice called out.

"Hi Doc." She greeted Doc Spencer as they both watched a police car pull up in the space next to hers. Matt Bradford stepped out. Opening the back door of his cruiser, he let two dogs out.

"Hi Doc," Matt greeted the vet. Then turning he said, "Hi Sandi," tipping his hat.

"Well, good morning, Officer Matt. What brings you here this morning? Isn't that Mike's canine".

"Yes, Rex was running in the north woods last night. He's favoring his left hind foot so I wanted him checked out, and I also need to get Max's vaccinations"

"Well, let's have a look at him," The vet replied unlocking the front door. "Sandi, could you do the vaccination for Max?"

"Sure, come on boy," as she lead the police dog into one of the side rooms.

Doc lifted Rex onto an exam table in room A. "Okay, Up boy, ……Hmmm……unhuh…… Hmmm," muttering to himself before finally turning to Matt "Looks like Rex might have been closer to the dam, than the woods. He has cuts and scrapes everywhere but here in his hind foot he has a thorn embedded deeply in the pad. The flesh is pretty cut up. Looks like more than just a run, want to tell me anything?" the vet questioned Bradford, his eyes sparkling.

"Official business I'm afraid Doc." Knowing the old man's need for gossip…ah, not gossip, but town news—news not yet available to the public. Bradford did not want to say too much, but he could tell the vet that Mike had slipped and been injured. "Mike got too close the edge on river road, near the dam and the side gave way. He was hurt and Rex came to town to get help."

"Is He okay?" Doc Spencer questioned, he was always ready for the latest news about Harmony Falls, since he was being forced to retire for health

19

reasons, current news made him feel still in the loop. "I wouldn't want to see our finest laid up"

"He'll be okay, broke his ankle. They airlifted him to the hospital. "How about Rex? Can I pick him up after my shift today?"

"Sure, I'll fix him right as rain and back on his feet. You can pick him up this afternoon."

"Okay, thanks Doc," Bradford turned to go, then pausing at the door, lowered his voice "Doc, on the QT, what do you know about your new assistant?"

"She's a good assistant—the best I've ever had—she'll be the new vet after I retire. Has all the makings of a great veterinarian……Came from San Francisco."

That explains her wariness! San Francisco can be a tough crowd! Matt thought to himself, he waited, wanting more information—he wanted to know details—other details—personal details.

The aging vet man enjoyed seeing the officer hang on his every word before going on. Doc Spencer was not oblivious to the officer's interest in Sandi "She is in her mid-twenties and she is single if that is important…." The veterinarian's voice trailed off, winking at the officer, as he stifled a chuckle.

"Okay matchmaker, I've got to get to work. I'll pick up Rex after my shift ends."

"I'm not doing anything but, it's high time you settled down, Matt." Doc Spencer reminded him "Just don't want life to pass you by!"

"I get off at six p.m. tonight—will you still be open?" Matt asked, quickly changing the subject *why does everyone try to set me up?*

"I'll have Rex ready."

Leaving the vet's office, Bradford whistled for his canine partner, "Come on Max. Thanks Sandi."

"You're welcome," She smiled.

Hmmm, nice smile, sure warms the heart! He thought.

Chapter 4

The week had flown by so fast; it was Saturday before Sandi realized it. But when her sister, Tammy, phoned that morning to get a little shopping down, Sandi was ready in record time. Just a week before Christmas, the morning was starting out bright and sunny after last night's snowfall. It was the perfect day to shop for the holidays, as the two headed towards the first store.

"I always enjoy Christmas shopping when a fresh snow has fallen, and all of the stores have displays lit. The snow is clean and beautiful. There's just an excitement in the air."

"I know just what you mean, Tammy. Everything is so brightly decorated. Everyone's mood changes from dreary day-in/day-out doldrums to a cheerful excitement, especially the kids. By the way, have you told Bill yet?" Sandi asked her sister.

"No, I was at the doctor's office yesterday: they said they would call when they know something. I don't want to get his hopes up, if I am not…" wishfully her voice trailed off.

"Oh Tammy I just know you are! Pretty soon we'll be purchasing a baby layette instead of Christmas gifts. That'll be so much fun!"

"Ooooo, Sandi, look at that quilt!" Tammy stopped in front Macy's window. "Wouldn't that look great in the house you are purchasing?"

"Oh yes! I agree! I like the blues and greens in it! Is that a basket weave pattern? I like the quilt next to it. Either one would be striking against the dark wood of my new spool bed. I could paint the walls a faint pastel green and let the colors of the quilt pick up on the wall color. Let's go in and see how much they want for it."

"Excuse me, Miss, Are the quilts made locally?"

"I believe so." The young lady looked twelve to Sandi.

"How much are they?"

Checking the price tag the saleslady told her.

"Good, I'll take this one."

After purchasing her new quilt, Sandi and Tammy left Macy's, loaded with gifts, unable to see around the packages, they were carrying.

"Hold on there, Ladies. Let me help hold open the door for you. Looks like your arms are full!" Peeking around the packages, Officer Bill smiled, bent down and kissed his wife, Tammy. Mischievously, winking at his sister in law, He teased "You wouldn't be helping by beautiful wife spend all our hard earned money, would you? Looks like there's enough here for at least half of the county."

Without missing a beat Sandi responded, "I am not aware of any current law regarding the appropriation or amount of money spent on Christmas for loved ones, Officer Brown! I would not dream of breaking the law."

"Well now, there just might be a law about that! I'd better call for back up!"

Tammy giggled and turned to her younger sister. "I guess we're busted Sandi. We had better head for home, besides we need to get ready for tonight's snowflake parade! Officer Brown, would you mind assisting us to our car? No peeking at gifts!"

"Me?! I would not dream of it!" Officer Brown feigned innocence. Putting the packages in the car the sisters headed towards Tammy's home

"I can't wait till tonight. I'm so excited to see the parade," Sandi exclaimed.

"It is quite beautiful, but dress warmly. It can get cold!"

Chapter 5

The annual snowflake parade was one of the town's hundred year old holiday traditions. Local legend told of a time when the town was first established, a young boy was lost in a snow storm on Christmas Eve: the townsmen had gone searching for the boy. The women folk had lit a bonfire so that the rescuers and the lad could find their way home. At the end of the today's parade the mayor of Harmony Falls, carrying a torch, will light the Yule fire, in the center of Veteran's Park.

Parking was hard to find, the two sisters ended up three blocks away and walking toward the parade. Sandi could hear the noise of an excited crowd. Refreshment carts had been set up at intervals along the route, selling hot chocolate and coffee, to warm those who were too cold.

The mayor and his wife were the first to appear as they sat in a red convertible, top down, waving to the crowd. As they passed, each street light was lit signifying the start of the parade.

Above the noise of the excited crowd, you could hear the drum roll of the High School band, looking festive in red and white uniforms, marching to the tune of Jingle bells and Deck the halls. Flag girls held their flags aloft performing in sync to the merry tunes. *I wondered how they stay warm dressed like that!* Sandi wondered. *I'm cold just thinking about it!*

There were many floats, but the crowds' favorite was the Macy's float. It looked like a scene from the North Pole with Santa's sleigh lit up in white lights. Children were seated on either side of Santa as he "flew" down the street in his sleigh. Elves, dancing behind, were tossing candy into the crowds of children who shrieked in delight to the sugary treat. The candy land float was another crowd pleaser with an array of candy canes lining a "path". There were the snowflake dancers dressed in life size snowflakes costumes dancing down the street to the tunes of "Let it Snow". The Old Time Jazz Band came next seated in the back of a pickup playing a jazzed version of traditional holiday music. Sandi's favorite float was the fire engine: sitting on top of the highly polished engine was the mascot, a Dalmatian named Spot.

"Thought I might find you out here. Are you enjoying the parade?"

Sandi turned to see Matt Bradford in his crisp blue uniform, and a heavy overcoat keeping a watchful eye on the crowd, his canine, Max, at his side.

"Oh Yes, It's quite beautiful!" Sandi answered.

"Can I buy you a cup of hot chocolate or coffee?"

"Yes, Thanks! Do you know my sister Tammy?" she introduced him.

"Yes, Bill's wife, around here everyone knows everyone. Part of the charm of Harmony Falls."

"That's right! How silly of me to forget. I'm still kind of used to San Francisco where you easily get lost in a crowd." She blushed.

"How is your brother?" Tammy asked.

"Mike is mending nicely. Thanks for asking." Turning to Sandi, Matt smiled "Easy enough to forget the charm of Harmony Falls if you're not used to it yet."

The three were chatting away when the police radio crackled to life. "10 adam 4 meet officer brown at 1164 Pine Street. We have a four-nine-five."

Bradford excused himself. "I'll love to stay and chat but duty calls. Enjoy the rest of the evening."

Heading towards Pine Street, Matt Bradford answered the call as he walked away.

"A burglary? Are you sure?"

"Yes, Officer Brown is on the scene."

"Copy that, I'm in route now" Bradford radioed.

After he left, Tammy turned to her sister and said, "You like him, don't you?"

"No! Yes! No! You are dreaming my dear sister" she laughed "Let's go, it's starting to snow again! And my toes are cold or numb from compression—wearing too many sox!"

"Well, He defiantly likes you!"

"I doubt that! He's just being polite. Tammy, you have had too much hot chocolate and it has gone to your head! I am not interested in a relationship right now. You know I do not want to go thru that again, besides it's been too soon." Sandi stated emphatically, "I am just not ready" *He is quite the gentleman,* she thought to herself. *I thought someone else was too, but he was just putting on a show, an act. Of course that was what I wanted to see too. How do I know that Matt's behavior is genuine and not just an act? I don't want to be beaten or have a knife pulled on me again. I don't want to be hurt again. No, it's better to be safe! No, no more relationships for me! This move is just what I need, period!*

Chapter 6

"Evening Bill, what do we have here?" Matt Bradford questioned as he walked into the Miller's home that night.

"The Millers came home from the parade to find their door standing wide open. Sylvia noticed some of her jewelry is missing and Mark is missing his hunting rifle," Officer Bill Brown informed him.

As Bradford walked over to the couple, Mark was comforting his wife. "Hi folks, I'm sorry this has happened tonight."

"Matt, we just never thought to lock our house. We've lived in Harmony Falls all of our lives and never had a problem, never worried about it. Harmony Falls has always been a nice place to live. We were just out enjoying the parade."

"I know Mark, Sylvia, It is a sad day when town folk have to start worrying about their safety.

Is anything else missing?'…besides the rifle and jewelry?" he added.

"I…I…I just…I don't think so," Sylvia stammered.

"Can you describe the jewelry?"

"Yes, One piece is my mother's silver broach. Two gold rings, one with a princess cut diamond and three sapphires on one side. The other ring had a large teardrop aquamarine stone and matching necklace. I have several necklaces with gold chains. My pearls are gone. Everything's gone, Matt, all of it. This is just awful. You will catch them won't you?"

"Yes, we will Sylvia, What was the rifle?"

"A 30-06, Smith and Wesson."

"Alright Mark, Sylvia, I need you both to sit down and write out a description of each piece, including the rifle. Do you have any pictures of the items? One last thing, I'll need to dust for prints."

"Anything you need Matt, just let us know."

"I'll let you get started on the descriptions, I'll check back in a little while." Bradford met up with Officer Brown outside "Bill, what did you find out here?"

"Not much Matt, There are no footprints under any of the windows. And there are too many prints from the parade onlookers out front. It looks like they just walked right up to the front door and walked in. Another thing—Mark stated that he kept the rifle in the back of his closet. No one would look in the back of a closet behind hanging clothes for a gun unless they knew it would be there. It's not a usual place to look for a rifle. Someone just passing thru town wouldn't know to look there. They would go for something quick and assessable like the jewelry. This looks to be a local job."

"Are you thinking of the Collins kid? He's only stolen small stuff so far. The rifle has me worried. Did he plan to use it or sell it?" Matt replied, thinking of the hunter found in the woods a few days ago.

"Yeah, that has me worried too. Did you see him in the parade tonight?"

"Yes, I did. He was with a few of the other high school boys. I better get back, if trouble is brewing. You'll finish here? I'll see if Philip Collins is still at the parade or if he's left. I'll check back with you later."

Chapter 7

Matt drove over to Mike and Cindy's home. "Hi! Thought I would shovel the sidewalks for you. How's the ankle doing?"

"Pretty Good, Doc says I'll be back to work in four weeks. I can't wait! This sitting around is driving me nuts! A man is just not meant to do nothing!"

"And me too!" Cindy chimed in. "I can't get anything done. All these doctor appointments. I no sooner start the laundry, then it's time for another appointment of one kind or another, each doc sends you out to two or three more doctors. Oh my, it is exhausting!"

"Well, we sure miss you at the office. Will they recommend desk work for a while?" Matt questioned.

"Probably, but I have several weeks of therapy ahead of me, then I'll know after that. They are talking about light duty for several months, but it depends on what the therapist determines. How's your cold?"

"Okay I guess, as long as I take cold medicine. That's the price I pay for getting you out of a jam! You owe me pal. You owe me double for shoveling your walks too!"

"Well, you can collect when I am back on my feet!"

"Oh, I will! Trust me, I will. Well, let me clear the sidewalk for you then I'm headed home to bed."

"Okay, Thanks, I owe you big time. How about dinner tonight?" "Thanks for the offer, but I'll take a rain check. I'm just beat."

"Alright, later then. Thanks for the shoveling."

"Uncle Matt!" The little blonde four year old lad raced into his uncle's arms "Uncle Matt, can we go play ball? Can we?"

"Not tonight Trevor. I need to go home." Matt adored his nephew. The lad had endless energy. "Sorry pal, I need to feed Max. How about you come over this weekend, I have the weekend off and we can have pizza, play ball, watch cartoons, okay?"

"I want to play ball now, I tried to play with Mom" the lad leaned in close to his uncle's ear and whispered "Mom throws like a girl! She doesn't even play snow ball right!" disappointment shone in the four year old's eyes.

33

"I'll tell you what, you can spent the whole weekend at my house, I'm sure the snow will still be around so we can baseball in the snow."

"Alright." Trevor reluctantly agreed. "Can we have cheese pizza?"

"We sure can!" Matt smiled, "Now give me a hug so I can go home."

Chapter 8

"Somehow Monday morning comes way too early in the morning" Matt complained to his police dog as he slowly climbed out of bed. "I wish we could just sleep in on Mondays. I sure am glad someone invented coffee and donuts. Speaking of donuts…I think it is my turn to… but…let me check…Yes, yes it is my turn. Guess, we'll have to stop at Dunkin Donuts."

After a quick shower, Matt stopped in at the pastry shop then on to the police station, where he met Detective White in the station's kitchen.

"Morning Matt." White greeted him. "Are you visiting Mike tonight?"

"Good Morning, Tom. No, not tonight pal, I have a date."

The detective raised his eyebrows "You? A confirmed bachelor?"

"Not confirmed, just not attached."

"Who's the lucky young lady?"

"Bill's wife has a younger sister who has moved to town recently."

"Isn't she the new vet assistant, Sandi, who works at Doc Spencer's?"

"Yeah" Matt felt a bit of pride.

"Where are you taking her?"

"We are going to a church Christmas program tonight."

"Is this a first date?'

"Yes"

"Hmmm, nice safe date."

"Thanks for your approval," Matt answered sarcastically.

"Anytime! Good Luck! I'll see you later then," The detective snickered as he left.

Matt turned back to the coffee pot and poured himself another cup. *A guy asks a gal on one date and the whole town has to have some say in the matter!* Deep in thought Matt hadn't noticed Officer Bill come in the room.

"Thanks for the donut, Matt, breakfast of champions! Don't let my wife know about them though; I promised her I would diet. She wants me to lose twenty pounds." Officer Bill took a bite of his donut "I see you are going over all your notes too. I have been going over mine also—nothing seems to make any sense. I'm going out to the Collins' home, then, check with the Millers' about the items missing."

"Okay, I'll drive, you eat!" Matt said. "By the way, I was always under the opinion that food not eaten at home does not count against a diet. I believe there is a law about that!"

"I like that thought, but I don't think Tammy will agree. I'm sure she'll shoot holes in that theory." Bill replied.

The two officers drove up the Collin's driveway. Tom Collins, a lean man in his forties, was bent over his truck's engine compartment, trying to get it to start.

"Morning Tom, problems with the truck again?" Matt asked, knowing the answer. It was always good to start this conversation with a few pleasantries.

"Hi Matt, Bill."

"Tom, we need to talk to your son. Is he around?" Matt asked.

"Yeah, that lazy son of mine is still in bed. What has he done this time?"

"We just want to talk to him, right at this time. Can we do this inside?" Matt asked.

"Yeah, come on in." Tom said, irritation rising in his voice, as he led them inside. Tom's wife, Stacy, looked up in alarm as soon as she saw the two officers. "Tom, what's wrong?" She questioned her husband, worried.

"We'll soon find out." **Phillip get out here, the police are here to see you!"** Tom yelled. Seconds later Phillip appeared in pajama bottoms, hair uncombed, half asleep. He sat down on the sofa.

"Boy, these officers are here to see you and you had better tell the truth." Tom demanded.

"Good Morning Phillip; Can you tell me where you were last night?"

"I was at the parade." Phillip answered sleepily.

"Is there anyone who was with you the entire time and could vouch for you?" Matt questioned.

"Yeah the whole town."

"Anyone specific we could talk to?" Matt continued.

"I told you, the whole town!" Phillip answered, his voice rising.

"You had better treat these officers with respect, boy," his father sternly warned him.

"You are not helping yourself son, give me a specific name we could talk to so we can confirm your whereabouts." Matt kept his voice level.

"I was with Robbie and Ryan White. You should know them. Their dad is on the police force with you." Phillip answered in a smug tone.

"Were you with them the entire evening?" Matt continued.

"Yeah, Pretty much."

"Did you go anywhere else, or go off by yourself at any time?"

"NO!" Phillip yelled.

"There's no need to get defensive unless you have something to hide. If you do, son, you had better let us know now, before this goes any farther." Matt advised.

"I don't even know what you are talking about."

"The Millers home was broken into. Do you know anything about it?"

"No, I told you I was with Robbie and Ryan the whole time"

"Have you used a rifle at any time recently?"

"No"

"Did you use a rifle to go hunting or just shooting at any time in the past thirty days?"

"No"

"How about in the past sixty days" Matt questioned further.

"NO, I told you NO!" Phillip's voice rising again.

"No need to raise your voice unless you have something to hide. Is there something else you need to tell us? Are you telling us the whole truth?" Bradford asked.

"I don't know anything about a rifle or the Millers. I was with Robbie and Ryan. Ask them."

"Okay, Thanks for your time Phillip. Tom, Stacy, have a good day." Taking their leave Matt and Bill got into the squad car. "Phillip seems very adamant about his statement. Let's go talk to

Robbie and Ryan White." Matt surmised. "See if they can verify his statement"

As they drove up the White's driveway, they saw Nancy in the front yard shoveling snow off the walk. Seeing the cruiser pull up, she set the shovel aside, "Hi," she greeted them.

"Morning Nancy, How are you today?" Matt greeted her.

"Good, thank you. Bob is not home right now, but you know that. Can I help you?" she asked.

"Yes, we wanted to talk to Robbie and Ryan. Are they home?"

"Yes. Robbie, Ryan." She called "These officers want to talk to you."

When the two boys approached, Bill pulled Robbie aside and questioned him as Matt talked to Ryan up on the porch. "Were you at the parade last night?"

"Yes" answered the fifteen year old trembling. He looked more like a scared child than a teenager; It was obvious that he had never been in trouble with the law.

"All night?"

"Yes sir"

"Who was with you?"

"Phillip Collins and Dan Wilson and my brother."

"Anyone else?" the officer persisted.

"No, just the four of us."

"Were you together the entire time? Did Phillip leave you at any time to go off by himself?" Matt asked watching the boy's responses.

"Phillip was with us the whole time."

"Did any of you go off to shoot a rifle, say just for fun?"

"No."

"Are you sure? Now is the time to let us know if you done anything or if Phillip has done or said anything." Matt said.

"No, He didn't say anything to us."

"Okay, Ryan. Thank you." Matt felt satisfied for the moment. Walking back to where Nancy stood, Matt informed her "I just needed to check on one of the high school boys. Thanks Nancy."

Getting back into the cruiser, Matt drove slowly down the drive. "Seems like Ryan can confirm Phillip's story."

"Robbie was able to verify his story also." Bill said. "Looks like we might have a unknown perpetrator and not Phillip."

"Yeah." Matt agreed, a growing uneasiness began to gnaw at him. He couldn't quite put his finger on it.

"His alibi seems to be iron clad. Let's check to see if the coroner's report can shed any light on this case." A heavy snowfall began as Matt drove back to the station in silence, each officer lost in his own thoughts.

Chapter 9

The snow had stopped for the moment, leaving another eighteen inches of snow to deal with. Pastor Jones, wearing a heavy coat and gloves, was outside shoveling the church's stairs and sidewalks. "Hi, Matt and Sandi" He greeted them "This snow will be good for the water levels next summer, but right now it is a mess and hard to keep everything clear."

"Yes, it is. Want help?" Matt asked him.

"No, go on inside and find a seat." Pastor replied. "I'll be done in a minute"

"I'll just go get my shovel out of my car and help. You'll get done faster and be able to enjoy the evening too. Be right back."

"He's a good man, Sandi. Considerate too." Pastor Jones commented. "Why don't you go one inside and find seats. No sense in you getting cold also. Don't forget to get a program and candle." Blushing, Sandi smiled as she thought about his comment to her.

The deep smell of heather pine filled the air as Sandi entered the church. Fresh cut evergreen trees lovingly adorned with the hand crafted ornaments the children in the church created, stood in the corner. Each ornament was as individual as the kids themselves, and beautiful in its own right. A manger scene was set up on stage. White twinkling lights simulating the starry night sky hung from the ceiling above. The sweet scent of hay created the atmosphere of a Bethlehem manger, mixed with the heather scent of pines, filled the sanctuary.

Finding a seat, she was deep in thought…*Matt seems nice, everyone likes him… and he was a gent…*

"Hi, Sandi," Tammy sitting down next to her, interrupted her thoughts, grinning ear to ear, glowing.

"Let me guess, your doctor confirms you are pregnant! You are beaming ear to ear!"

"Yes I am! But don't say anything yet; I have not had a chance to tell Bill. He doesn't get off till midnight tonight. He's going to be so excited! I can't wait to tell him!"

"Any ideas on what colors and theme you want for the baby's room?"

"Yes, I was thinking about a pale green and white and maybe a Noah's ark theme. Want to come over and help me paint? I am going to move Bill's office upstairs and have the nursery next to our bedroom. But I will have to do a lot of cleaning and painting. Can I get Auntie Sandi to make a quilt?'"

"Of course! We could make the quilts together. This will be so exciting. Have you told Mom and Dad yet?"

"No, I'll tell them after I spring the news to Bill, and I do not know how to make quilts, so you'll have to teach me."

"I'll show you how, it's really quite easy. Oh, I get to sign the papers for the house tomorrow. I am so excited!" Sandi exclaimed. "I was hoping you could help me pack and Bill could help move. I was going to ask Matt to help me move also. Oh, the program is starting. Call me, after you have told Bill. We'll make plans later."

Chapter 10

January in Harmony Falls usually had a lot of snow, but this year, they had that amount and more, setting a new record. This day was no different as it dawned to another heavy snow fall, making the move into her new home difficult. But, after signing the papers at the real estate office, that bitter cold January morning, she excitedly picked up her keys and started moving in. She just couldn't wait for it to stop snowing, to move in. It took her awhile to find her boots and a heavier coat, before venturing outside to clear the driveway of her newly purchased home.

Shoveling a few feet, she stopped for a breath and looked around in awe at the beauty of the fresh snow. A fresh blanket of snow laying on top of bare branches, dressed the trees in glistening elegance. Shriveled, brown weeds left from last year's growth stood above the stark white snow, heavily laden with ice crystals, resembling an exquisite fine necklace strung with shimmering diamonds, its beauty, breathtaking. The winter sun reflecting on the glistening ice crystals, shone brightly through each diamond.

"Snow is beautiful on treetops, lawn and rooftops, but it is terrible to shovel off the driveway!" Sandi complained to herself as she set to the task again.

Noticing her new home looked a little forlorn without any curtains at the windows, Sandi thought, *I could make some blue curtains for the living room and they would make the place look homey and inviting. I wonder if Macy's has curtains that I would like? Hmmm, I could get a welcome wreathe for the front door, kind of cheer the place a little. I saw one at that little craft shop! Now that Tammy is going to have a baby, I will be able to have the baby shower in my new home, if I ever find the floor. I like the sound of my home……my home……mine! That feels just so…so… delicious!* Sandi smiled. *My home! I like the sound of that!*

Every muscle in Sandi's body ached from shoveling the heavy snow, as she stopped to watched a car struggle up the driveway. The brilliant bright sunlight was making it hard to see. "Morning Sandi" Matt called as he stopped the car and got out, wearing jeans and a sweatshirt.

Every time she saw Matt she felt mixed emotions. *He seems nice and sincere, but so did someone else at first… Is he really sincere? Or is this just a game? Am I blind because I want to see these qualities in him or are these qualities he really possesses? Heavenly Father, can I trust him? Please give me wisdom, Lord.*

"Can I help you shovel?" He asked as he walked up.

"Yes, Thanks! Bill will be here soon with a pickup load of things and I wanted to make it easier to move stuff inside."

"Why don't you go in and warm up some, while I finish clearing this."

"Okay, I think I might be able to find my teapot and make some hot tea. Would you like some?" She asked.

"Yes, I would. Thanks."

Inside Sandi removed her wet snow boots, and searched for her teapot. Finally unable to find her tea pot; Sandi heated some water in a saucepan, then searching through the boxes she had already moved in, she located some cups and tea bags. Waiting for the water to boil, she watched Matt shoveling outside, *He sure is a thoughtful person and he definitely is not a lazy individual either. I wish I could trust my feelings, one minute I really like him and the next……. Please, help me Lord. What should I do?*

Making a cup of tea for Matt, Sandi put back on her boots and went outside.

"Here, I don't have any sugar yet," as she handed him the piping hot tea. His hands brushed against hers sending shivers down her spine. Looking up she knew he felt the same electricity between them as he smiled down at her. "That's fine" his voice a little husky. A honk from Bill truck bought the two of them back to the present.

"Ummm, Bill is here with the truck." She said weakly, needing to break the connection she was feeling…… a connection she wasn't sure she wanted to encourage.

"Hey, you two." Bill and Tammy greeted them as they drove up to the house. Bill and Matt started unloading the truck, Sandi held the door open as they brought her furniture inside, giving instruction as to where to place each piece. "Tammy just informed me last night that we will be adding to our family!" Bill announced grinning ear to ear.

"Congratulations!"

"We are so excited!"

"That's great! If you need help painting or something, let me know. Grab that end of this dresser and we'll take this inside next. Okay?" Navigating the heavy dresser up the threshold stairs Matt joked "Where to my lady?"

"Upstairs, first door on the left will be the master bedroom" Sandi instructed. After a day of many trips in and out, the truck was empty. Sandi was thankful that she could finally close the front door and turn up the heat! She began to put things away, when Matt and Bill brought her a load of fire wood and stacked the kindling next to the back door for easy access. "Oh my goodness I did not expect this! Thank you both!" She exclaimed.

"A housewarming gift from Tammy, Bill, and Myself." replied Matt as he stacked a few logs by the fireplace. "I know you are tired from moving all day, so how about I take you out to dinner?"

"How about a pizza here?" she suggested. "I'm bushed."

"Sounds fine to me." He agreed "Do you like pepperoni?"

"Yes, I do."

"Fine, I'll order. Bill, you and Tammy care for some pizza?" Matt asked.

"No Tammy is worn out and well, three's a crowd, or four in our case. Think we'll bow out…" Bill answered grinning. "See you later."

Chapter 11

Sandi answered her door the next morning; Matt was standing there with a box in his arms. "Hi, Matt." She yawned.

"I would have called first, but you don't have a phone yet, I hope you're' planning on having one installed soon."

"I'm just going to use my cell phone right now . What's in the box?" She yawned again, irritated at the early arrival. "What time is it anyway?"

"Almost 10:30. You slept in a little."

"Hmmm, I guess I did! I kept on unpacking late last night after you left. Why don't you come in?" She was starting to feel more comfortable with Matt around, *I guess if anyone tried to bother me, it would help to have an officer of the law hanging around a lot. I don't have to marry the man, just let him be seen hanging around. It can't hurt to have a little protection, especially after San Francisco.*

"I brought you a dog to keep you company and also help protect you. And I picked up dog food and a leash." He said as he handed her a box, then going back to his car, produced a black pup, full of energy.

"Why, he's just a pup!" She exclaimed.

"Don't worry, He'll grow out of it soon!" Matt answered trying hard not to laugh.

"Everyone is a comedian." she replied giggling.

She was grateful that he looked out after her, *Kind of makes me feel safe, and well after......him. It would look better to have a cop hanging around.*

"Well, I work today so I'll be seeing you. But ......would you like to go out to dinner tonight?" Matt asked.

"Yes, I would" she replied unable to believe she had agreed so readily. *After all,* She reasoned. *she did need the relationship to look serious if she was to scare "him" away.*

"Great, I'll pick you up at seven o'clock. I get off at six. See you then." Getting back in his car, Matt drove to work, whistling, feeling like he was the luckiest man is the world.

Chapter 12

Sandi came in as usual on Saturday to clean the office. During the week she ended up being just too busy, so she normally came in on the weekend for an hour or so to clean, organize, file, refill sanitizers, and feed any pets that were being boarded.

It was during her cleaning, she found it, a little cardboard box on the top shelf of a book case, in the very back. She had seen it there before, but didn't pay any attention. Today, though, she had time to find a ladder and retrieve it. The box was dusty, Opening it carefully she found it contained a dozen or so cassette tapes and a recorder. *Curious*, she thought. *Why would he keep this up here? And what are these tapes?*

Nervously looking around she checked to make sure she was alone, although she knew she was, still she felt guilty, like she was committing a

crime. Popping a cassette into the tape recorder Sandi pressed play……nothing happened.
*Hmmm… no power. L*ooking for an on/off switch she noted it was already on. Searching the box Sandi found an electric cord and plugged the tape recorder in. Immediately, she heard Doc's voice.

- Today we had an elderly couple come in with their little dog, cute little fellow. As always, I engaged them in conversation, trying to get to know them. New to the area, they relayed this story…

- "In their early 20's they lived in a rural town. The town was fortunate enough to have a twenty bed hospital and a veterinary office. The veterinary office was too small to do any surgical procedures, so if any were needed, say on a pig for example, they would just take the animal to the hospital. The resident doctor would do blood work, x-rays, and the vet would operate right in the hospital."

- "Today Sally brought in her cat. She has trained the cat to sit, come, stay, and even fetch a ball. She brought in a ball to demonstrate.

Named the cat Velcro. Good owner, smart cat!"

- "Today someone brought in a golden retriever they found wandering up by the dam, I don't recognize her as belonging to anyone, if no one claims her in a few weeks, I might just take her home with me. I was filing in the back room, when the phone rang, by the time I turned to answer the phone, that dog had picked it up off the receiver and brought it to me! Of course it was slimy. She is the most endearing dog!"

- "The little Johnson boy brought in his Sheltie today, the boy and dog have both learned their 123's. Craziest thing I ever saw! There was the dog—you could ask him to find a "3" and the dog could find it! Even bark the right number of times! I've never seen anything like it in all my years as a vet! Sometimes the boy could find the number before the Sheltie! The Johnson lad is recovering nicely; Those two are quite a pair! I don't know who is rescuing who, but they both are good for each other."

The stories went on and on, dozens of stories over the past forty years, each tape containing more stories of the funny antics of animals, and the way each one interacted with their owner, some funny, some serious, each clip demonstrating the love of man and beloved pet.

Wonder what he was going to do with all these tapes, these stories are wonderful! He could write a book! These are absolutely wonderful!

Giggling thru the next story a thought formed in Sandi's head. *Hey, I could have these typed up for Doc! He might enjoy these after he retires! Wonder who in town does this kind of dictation, I could do it myself in a pinch, but I would be slow at it. Some of these sound like just treatment notes. I'll have to check with the typist he used to go to.*

Chapter 13

February fourteenth, a day set aside to honor
lovers around the world, was just another day to
Sandi. A sad day. A day that reminded her of the
failure of her marriage. A day she would rather
ignore, a marriage she wished she could forget
ever happened, but that letter she had just received
had familiar handwriting.

Her stomach twisted in knots, and fear gripped
her heart as she stood staring at the writing. *How
could he find me here? I even changed my name
when I moved!* Terrified, she looked around,
imagining him behind every tree, spying on her.
Enraged, she threw the letter in the trash,
unopened, slamming the lid down firmly, fuming
she stormed toward her house. Pausing at the door,
she stopped and thought about it, the letter, she
could…*Yeah… that might do it… that might solve
her dilemma, Yes, that is what I'll do!* Resolved in
her plan of action, Sandi walked back to where the

trash cans were, looking around she checked to make sure no one was watching her after she had made so much noise. Retrieving the envelope out of the trash, she looked around again, hoping none of her neighbors saw her digging in the garbage. That would be embarrassing and complicated to explain! She didn't want anyone to know her secret.

Resisting the intense urge to shred the unwelcomed letter to pieces, to assuage her anger, she slide it in her pocket. Turning, she nonchalantly walked back up the stairs and unlocked her front door and went in, taking one last look to scan for any sign of an uncouth invader lurking behind a tree or bush.

Rummaging thru her desk, she couldn't find it, looking in another drawer she couldn't find it there either, looking in a third drawer, she finally found the big super fat marker she had been hunting for. Using her left hand to disguise her own handwriting, she wrote in bold letters; NOT AT THIS ADDRESS. Feeling gratified Sandi smiled, she would have the post office mark the envelope as undeliverable! That should stop him!

Getting in her car she enjoyed the euphoric feeling of satisfaction in emphasizing her position of independence. Stopping at Starbucks', she ordered a vanilla latte as a celebratory drink.
Arriving back home an hour later, Matt was waiting for her on the front porch.

"Hi!" she called cheerfully, getting out of her car, still feeling giddy about her recent success.

"Well, you're in a fantastic mood! Must have had a good day!"

"Pretty good overall! How about your day?"

"Not as great as yours. I brought you these. Happy Valentines!" holding up a red rose bouquet and box of chocolates, he waited in anticipation of her response, still unsure of his position with her. She seemed to appreciate him spending time at her home, but at times she seemed distant or even uninterested, almost to the point of aloofness. Seemingly vacillating between a casual friendship and true interest. He knew how he felt though, there was no doubt that he was head over heels in love. There was an electricity between them. He had felt it! He knew she had felt that same spark, he witnessed it in her eyes. It was obvious to him, a trained observer; she had a bad relationship somewhere, just by her wariness, even though she had never mentioned it. But, he was willing to wait, to give her time to heal, eventually trusting him, opening up to him. He would wait. *She is worth it! Yes, she is worth it! She is my pearl of great price! A blessing sent from above!*

Holding his breath as he stood there holding out his token of affection, he waited,... the wait felt like an eternity,... and there,... there was her smile, the smile shone in her eyes, then on her lips, melting his heart. A smile that He would give up his life for! Yes, He loved her! He was sure of that! He would wait patiently…for her.

Chapter 14

It had been a week since she had returned that letter, and there hadn't been any response, no one new snooping around town. No one asking embarrassing questions, no hint of the terrible secret she carried. She had been nervous the entire week, looking over her shoulder, imagining a shadow behind every corner, but nothing happened. Thank Goodness! Maybe, it was finally over, for good!

Starting to relax, she began to enjoy life again making plans to redo her kitchen. At the hardware store, she went in armed with pictures out of decorating magazines that had inspired her. Standing in front of the paint samples, she tried to envision colors and themes in her kitchen. *I have always enjoyed a blue kitchen, but somehow it doesn't fit this kitchen, this house, since I have stainless steel appliances, I wonder how that vineyard motif would look? I like those grape vine*

kitchen towels I saw. This looks sort of like the right burgundy purple color. And this looks like the right green, but I really don't want green as the main color. I really like that burgundy purplish color. It is so hard to see a whole room finished before you actually paint it. Learned that lesson the hard way when I painted the bathroom, I overdid that color. Thought that blue would be right and it is just too strong for the small room. Dark blue in a small bathroom –feels like a cave! I wish there was a computer program that shows me what I have chosen, before I actually do the work!
"Planning on painting?"

Startled, Sandi jumped! Looking at the elderly gentleman standing next to her as if he was an ogre.
"Oh, I'm sorry I startled you. Are you alright? You look like you have seen a ghost!"

She nervously glared at the sixty year old gentleman who addressed her wondering just who he was. Had his spy found her? Staring at this stranger, she felt like bolting from the store. Was he the store clerk or someone else? Was someone stalking her? Nervously, reeling in turmoil, she finally stammered cautiously "Y…Y…Yes, I… I'm trying to paint my kitchen, but I am having a hard time trying to see it in my mind's eye."

"Ahh, kitchens, can be quite tricky. My late wife and I painted ours. What a pain it was, but well worth the effort when we were finished."

"Do you have any advice? What mistakes to avoid?"

"Hmmm, let's see. You could paint half of a wall and see if you like the color for the next week, my other suggestion is whatever color you do choose, go several shades lighter. It always looks stronger when you have an entire wall covered." The kindly old gentleman recommended. "I really didn't mean to startle you, Miss."

"That's alright. Just a hard day I guess. I think that is what I did wrong the first time. I painted my bathroom a few months ago and it's just too dark, feels like a dark blue cave. I'm thinking of repainting it again!"

Laughing, he agreed "One project at a time huh. I did that one too."

"Yes, One project at a time." she agreed laughing "One more question. Does this look like the right burgundy or what do you think?"

"Well, if I might suggest, You could go a little more neutral, say a tan or beige shade, then bring in the other colors with pictures and kitchen towels, curtains maybe. At least if the kitchen doesn't turn out like you thought, then just rethink the accessories. The painting won't have to be done again."

"That is a really good idea. Thanks," Sandi said. "I'll take a gallon of this paint, in this color."

"Actually, I don't work here; I came in for paint myself."

"Oh!" Sandi exclaimed in surprise. "You seem so knowledgeable."

"Done a lot of painting in my time. The clerk is over there. I'll carry your paint to the counter, young lady. Well, good luck on your painting."

"Thank you." She answered softly, watching him leave, She needed to be more careful, he could have been......... "

"You're welcome." The man said chucking, tipping his hat, as he left.

After purchasing a few more supplies, she headed home, stopping at Starbuck's for a latte on her way. I guess I am just a little too nervous, maybe I need to lay off the caffeine!

Driving past a grocery store, she pulled in, remembering that she needed some dog food for Toby. *Might as well purchase something for tonight's dinner too. And I need some popcorn, as I'm out.*

Chapter 15

There had been no retaliation since she had returned the letter. It had already been two weeks. She stopped seeing an imaginary shadow around every corner and behind every tree after a month had gone by. Believing her ruse to be successful, Sandi relaxed. To celebrate, she drove into the big city to Olive Garden Restaurant. Her favorite place to eat! She was finally rid of that lout and that was cause enough to celebrate!

An elegant dinner in a nice restaurant sounded like the perfect triumph to end that miserable existence she had left behind! A great way to celebrate out-smart that hooligan.

Since Matt had to work, she went alone. She wasn't even sure how to explain it to him anyway. Besides, it's not like they were married or anything. She certainly didn't owe him any explanations. She wouldn't even know where to start with <u>that</u> story! Besides, she just won the argument; she stated her position, isn't that why she was out celebrating? She had the last word, the final say! That chapter was ended, so why relive it or even explain it?

Pulling into the parking lot, she parked her car, being sure to lock it. Over the past month she had developed that habit, now it seemed like just a natural process. *The habits we learn out of necessity.*

Looking around, she breathed in deeply, at times she missed the big city life of San Francisco with the ambiance and night life. Harmony Falls seemed to roll up its sidewalk about six p.m. each evening. Sometimes she missed that part of city life! That, and the shopping. Harmony Falls had a wonderful small town feel, but sometimes good choices were limited. As the waitress escorted her to a seat, Sandi ordered the lobster, salad and Ice Tea. As she waiting for her meal, she looked around, just to be sure. It doesn't hurt to be extra careful. She didn't want trouble to find her away from home.

The waitress came with her meal. The salad was just divine. Every mouthwatering morsel was incredible, and it just melted in her mouth. Olive Garden made the best salad and lobster, bar none. *Boy, I sure missed the fine dining.* Sandi enjoyed her triumphant meal.

Chapter 16

Sandi arrived at Tammy's dressed in old jeans and a sweatshirt. "Ready?" she asked.

"Yes, but this morning sickness is awful!" Tammy complained as she came out of the bathroom, still a little green.

"Have you eaten yet?"

"No, I will in a minute or two." Tammy sighed as she plopped down in a kitchen chair. "It's too hard to eat when you have just urked. Besides, food does not sound good at all right now."

"Well, you do have to eat. Why don't I fix you some breakfast. Want eggs or oatmeal?" Sandi offered.

"Okay, but give me a moment. Let my stomach settle first."

"I thought the morning sickness was supposed to ease up by now." Sandi commented.

"It was supposed to, but I am just past three months." Tammy complained.

"Did you ask the doctor? We don't have to paint today, if you don't feel up to it." Sandi offered.

"No, I'll paint today, just takes a while to feel up to it."

"Alright, I'll make us some coffee and toast. Did you decide on which motif you wanted for the nursery?" Sandi asked.

"Yes, I like the Noah's Ark pattern; I'll need you to show me how to make a quilt. Maybe next week or so we go to the fabric store."

"That would be fine, just let me know when." Sandi said.

"Well, ready to paint? Bill moved that office furniture upstairs so all we have to do is paint and decorate. I bought some lace curtains that are kind of frilly but they have a rainbow pattern, which would go with the Ark theme. I was also thinking of printing verses, framing them and hang on the wall with this ribbon. What do you think?" Tammy said holding up a pretty light green ribbon smiling. "I'll print the verses on the computer. Could you paint these frames white? Here's the frames and paint."

"Oh, that would be lovely!" Sandi agreed.

They spent the morning painting and decorating in anticipation of a new family member. Each brush stroke of color applied with love as they transformed the room into a nursery fit for a little blessing!

Chapter 17

The first day of spring! And it felt like it! The sky was a brilliant blue. The late March morning sun spreading its warmth, melting the winter snows, creating a muddy mess of the landscape. Sandi's front yard had a few bulbs starting to peek their heads above the ground *March comes in like a lion and goes out like a lamb, I hope it just stays mild, I am so sick of snow. Besides I am enjoying seeing everything spring to life! Oh, little bulbs coming up, looks like daffodils I hope they will be the little yellow and white ones.* The Lilac and Forsythia bushes were just starting to bud and the roses weren't far behind. In back of her house, in the orchard, fruit trees were starting to bud also. *I love spring with all the pretty little flowers, all the new growth. It just feels so alive! So fresh! So new!* Matt had been coming over to help with different projects around the house. Sandi was enjoying these home projects. Sometimes they were projects she needed done and sometimes he came up with a few ideas. They both had grown fond of each other over the past four months. Sandi slowly had begun to let her defenses down. It hadn't been easy, but she had learned to trust him, to rely on him, and in turn, she filled a void in his life.

....

Matt also was enjoying spending time with Sandi over the past few months, he felt like he had found something that he had been missing. It brought back fond memories of his parents. Of the house he had grown up in. His Mom always had a large garden with plump, ripe tomatoes that she canned every year, along with strawberries, and sweet crunchy carrots. She could make the best pies and jams. She had won first place for her chokecherry jam at the fair one year. He missed his parents—for a time, but after a while the pain had lessened. Now, it seemed like all that might change. Matt found himself patrolling Sandi's neighborhood often just to keep an eye on her, keep her safe, although she seemed quite capable. He felt he wanted to protect her, to hold her. He found himself wanting to spend more time with her, craving her companionship. *I wonder if she feels the same about me.* He sighed, *Would she want to be with me forever? It is too soon to be feeling like that* he chided himself. *We've only known each other four months.*

As fulfilled as Matt felt in his relationship with Sandi, it was equal to the frustration he felt in not having solved the murder and burglary cases that were piled on his desk *(If you can call two cases a pile).* The heavy snows over the past winter had slowed the investigation. He felt like the cases were as cold as the frigid winter itself. There were few leads and the only real suspect to the burglary had three credible alibis. Robbie and Ryan White, also Dan Wilson. Each of those teenagers were reliable and trustworthy. Matt was glad to see Phillip Collins had started to hang around with more reputable kids, but that did not help the officer in determining what had transpired.

There had been dozens of visitors to Harmony Falls for the holidays last winter, but none seemed to have any involvement in either case. The fingerprints they had pulled from inside the Millers home had been run thru AFIS with no results. The stolen gun had not shown up in any of the local pawn shops either. There was no sign of the missing jewelry anywhere-like these items had just fallen off the face of the planet.

The coroner's report had confirmed that the victim Raymond Wills had died from a gunshot wound to the chest, no surprise there. The striation of the bullet did not match anything on file. Matt had contacted the family of Mr. Wills last winter. The family had filled out a missing person's report when the hunter had not returned home. They felt the deceased did not seem to have any enemies. *Why would anyone steal a rifle from the Millers' to kill the hunter? What was the connection?* Sitting pensively at his desk, Matt was going over his notes, when Mike Bradford walked in, using a cane, his canine by his side.

"Morning."

"Good Morning Mike, I see you are upgraded to a cane now. How is your ankle?"

"Doing well. Doc says I should be off the cane in a couple months or so. The pins that they used to set the bones don't seem to help my flexibility at all. The exercises aren't much better. Wouldn't do to have a cop with a cane chasing a bad guy!"

"No, that would look funny, I'm not sure anyone would take you seriously that way."

"Anything new on the cases?"

"No, I've contacted the family and they don't believe he was involved in any unscrupulous business. As far as they knew, He was just going hunting. They are not aware of any animosity towards him, and feel that he was loved by all who knew him. When he did not return they put out a missing person report. We released his body back to the family for burial. And...... let's see... the coroner's report did not bring up anything unexpected ...gunshot to the chest...... bullet retrieved was a 30-06." Matt replied.

"Hmm, the back side of the dam is a good place to off someone…secluded and all. Snow would cover any foot prints, animals to finish the job if needed. It seems odd to me that a hunter, especially a seasoned one would go hunting alone during the middle of winter……You always go with a buddy, in case of an accident." Mike stated thoughtfully, his voice trailing off.

"Yes, that is one of several oddities of this case," Matt replied thoughtfully.

"Bradford." Detective White called across the room.

"What?" The brothers answered in unison.

"A fax just came in. Looks like if might be one of the jewelry pieces and the rifle." White answered. "Here you are." Handing Matt the fax. "I have the list……somewhere…hmmm……ahh, here it is……Sure looks to be the same. I'll call Sylvia." Matt dialed the Miller's and leaning back in his chair as he waited for her to answer. "Sylvia?"

"Yes, this is Sylvia."

"Sylvia, this is Officer Matt Bradford, could you come down and identify a piece for us?

"You found my jewelry?!"

"We need both of you to identify these pieces for us, how soon could you be here?"

"I'll be down right away! Oh, thank you, I knew you would find it! Thank You!"

"Don't get too excited yet. We ......" click. Matt heard the dial tone.

In her excitement, Sylvia had already hung up. Waiting for Mark and Sylvia to arrive seemed to take an eternity, even though in reality only a few minutes had passed. Matt's thoughts were racing. *Was it possible that the perpetrators would steal a rifle from the Miller's use it to murder Raymond Wills, and then pawn it? That didn't make a lot of sense, but then crimes don't usually. Why not just drop the weapon in the lake side of the dam?*

The police station's front door flung open, slamming into the walls with a loud bang. Sylvia Miller rushed in, hair disheveled, cooking apron on, and house slippers still on her feet. She made a beeline for Matt Bradford's desk and breathlessly asked to see her jewelry.

"Sylvia, sit down first. Before we show you the photos, we don't actually have the pieces here; this information came over the fax. These are the pictures they have sent to us. Do these look like any of the pieces you have reported as being stolen?"

Sylvia took a deep breath then looked at the photo "Si, Si, that is my mother's brooch. See the little stone on the edge that is aquamarine, and this one here is a diamond. The diamond was for my sister, she was born in April, bless her heart, she is gone. And the aquamarine was for me, since I was born in March. Both my mama and my sister are gone now. This one here is a ruby for my brother He did not live long after he was born. That broke my mama's heart. I am so excited! When will they return my jewelry?"

"We'll need to contact the shop owner and confirm the find, then we'll make arrangements to have the property sent back here. That all takes time. We will call you when it is ready to be returned to you."

"Oh, I am so happy, that brooch means the entire world to me!" she exclaimed breathlessly. "We'll need Mark to come in as soon as he can to identify the rifle, alright?"

"Si, Si, I will let him know! Thank You!" True to her word, Sylvia and her husband Mark showed up after work that day, He was able to identify the rifle as the 30-06 taken from his home. The serial numbers matched.

With any luck, maybe we'll get this solved, and wrapped up. The sooner the better, then things can get back to normal. Matt thought.

"Matt, while you were talking to Sylvia, a man came in asking about your girlfriend's address. Said his name was Trayson. Know anything about this?"

"No, Sandi has not mentioned anything to me. Probably just a salesman selling veterinary supplies." Matt felt an odd mixture of jealousy and protectiveness. *Why didn't she tell me? Why should she? I'm just being a jealous old poo. Of course she will have salesmen coming to her place of business. If I need to know, she'll tell me. I trust her.*

Matt's weekend started with rototilling Sandi's garden. He still had the tiller that had belonged to his parents. He enjoyed doing things for Sandi, even when she wasn't home. *The one bad thing about being a policeman, I don't always get the same days off as other folks.* The ground was saturated with snowmelt, which made it easier to turn the soil, but still a little muddy. Later in the month he would till in a little cow manure, since the soil had not been worked before, Matt wanted to turn the ground early. Next year it will not be such a challenge. His mouth watered for the fresh vegetables they would harvest. He struggled to control the jerking machine as it bit deeply into the soft dirt, churning up the soil, that had been untouched for many years.

Stopping for a break, he wiped the sweat from his brow, daydreaming of picking the perfect succulent, ripe, red strawberry, slowly eating the tasty morsel, as it melted in his mouth, refreshing his senses in delicious sweetness. *I'll have to see if I have any of Mom's recipes for strawberry jam in the old box of papers, or maybe Mike has a copy.* Finishing the yard work, he put the weeds that he had pulled during rototilling in the trash, and that was when he saw it.... A letter... addressed to ...My Love Miss Sandi Johnson. It was wadded up

76

and thrown out. Noticing the return address—San Francisco. He also noticed a large bouquet of red roses...looked fresh. *Does she have another suitor?* Detective White's comment came flooding back "While you were talking to Sylvia, a Mr. Trayson asked her address."

Disturbed by what he found in the trash Matt decided he needed to clear the air but was unsure of how to broach the subject. *Hi! I was going thru your trash and found a love letter what's up? Yeah, that would go over well. No, I need to trust her that if there was someone else she would rather be with, she will talk to me. This is just a test of our love and commitment to each other.* Matt stored the tiller in Sandi's barn, and left for home, still thinking about those flowers in the trash. His stomach twisted in a knot, as he considered her "other suitor".

Chapter 18

Friday morning Matt went to work, expecting to find the cases solved, only to find out nothing was solved at all. The rifle had gone thru the crime lab and the bullets did not match the one that killed Raymond Wills. *I don't believe it! I thought we had found the weapon that killed Mr. Wills. This has to be the rifle. What am I missing! Why can't we find the guy who killed the hunter? Guess I'll start at the beginning and go thru everything again.*

Sitting down, Matt pulled out the file from his desk drawer. Opening it in exasperation Matt decided this would be better read with a donut and coffee. Putting the file back, he left for the donut shop and returned an hour later. Pulling the file out a second time, He started reading, searching for any answers, any clue, any hint, of what might have killed the hunter, how the jewelry fit into the crime, what really happened at the dam that cold winter's night last December? How the two incidences could, or could not be related. *WHAT AM I MISSING?! Why would anyone steal jewelry and a rifle, and then stop to kill the hunter? Did the hunter see something? Then try to stop a crime? No the hunter was found a few days earlier, so that can't be it. Why don't the bullets from the gun match to the bullet taken from the body of Mr. Wills? What am I missing? There has got to be something here, something that I didn't see at first. I think I'll take a drive out to the dam, the snow is melting with the weather being warmer now and I could look around the dam, the river, the surrounding brush although there is still some snow in the higher elevation, I should be able to retrace events. Maybe I can get a fresh perspective up there.* Matt took his canine, Max and headed out.

Chapter 19

After a frustrating day, Matt was ready for a nice quiet evening. "You look nice, did you get a haircut?" He asked when she answered the door.

"Yes, I did. I'm glad you like it. You seem down, anything wrong?"

"Mmm, a hard day at work, that's all," He answered.

"I'm sorry, we could just get pizza and relax at the house together instead of going somewhere," She suggested.

"That would be really nice. I'll start a fire in the fireplace and then order pizza." He answered, grateful that she understood. *That is one quality I really appreciate in her. She is thoughtful and considerate of others and their needs.* Bringing in some firewood, Matt built a fire, then sat back and watched the flames lick at the wood, curling around each log, biting into each piece, creating a controlled fury as it heated the room. *This is kind of mesmerizing to watch the fire burn. If I had not been able to be a policeman, I probably would have gone into firefighting, although it would be depressing to see a beautiful forest destroyed by a fire.*

"I have a few movies we could watch. Let me find the box they are packed in. I'll be right back." *Lord, I sure am blessed to have Sandi in my life. She's kind and compassionate. She loves you, Lord. We do have a lot of the same interests.* Matt prayed silently as he watched the fire burning in the fireplace.

Sandi returned with a movie and put in the machine, sitting next to him, she settled in to watch the movie.

She sure is beautiful, both inside and out, as he watched her sitting next to him, the desire to hold her was strong as he gently slid his arm around her, holding his breath. She looked up, nestled closer and smiled. *This feels so right, Lord. I would love to have her by my side.*

At the end of the movie, they talked into the night. Finally Matt asked her "Did I ever tell you about this house before you bought it?"

"No, No you haven't." she answered softly.

"The Fergusons, Ralph and Maddie Ferguson, lived here about sixty years, before they were married, Ralph had a small cabin right where the barns stands now. When He asked her to marry him, he built this house, just for her, put in the large kitchen, as she liked to cook. He tore down the cabin and built the barn. They had three children, their eldest fell thru the ice on the river, caught pneumonia and died shortly thereafter. Their second, a daughter, married and moved away...I think she moved to New York... or maybe it was New Jersey... I don't recall. The youngest son, John, was a year older than me. My brother, John and I would hang around together, he went in the military, unfortunately was killed in action. I can remember coming over, when we were kids and John's Mom would be baking up a storm, those were the best cookies! We would do homework here, and hang out in her kitchen, just to lick the bowl! Sure made the best place to study! Ralph would always take Maddie out on a date every Saturday night. John would come over to my house on those nights. You should have seen Ralph and Maddie, She would be wearing her fancy flowered hat, it had a little lace that came down over her eyes, and a nice fur coat. Ralph would always take her to the diner on Fifth and Main. Then after wards they would shop at Macy's, then onto the Ice Cream Shoppe. It was like clockwork, with those two. After she passed, I think it was cancer, Ralph just kind of... was... lost after that. Never went out any more...We stopped seeing him around town. He stopped working on the house. Stopped going to church. Just stopped living in general. There had so much sadness in their lives, but you could never tell, up until Maddie passed away. She was his whole life." Matt paused in his reminiscing

"That is so sad, but such a beautiful love story. You sure don't see many people married for sixty years anymore."

"No, No you don't" Matt agreed "I think part of that is society and part is just people."

"Did they have cattle in the barn?"

"Yes, cows and chickens"

"What about the orchard?"

"Well, that was Maddie's thing, cooking. She'd make all sorts of jams, jellies, Canned beans, corn. Won a few ribbons too!"

"What ever happened to her recipes?"

"I don't know, I was in college when she passed away, so I really didn't pay attention to things going on around me, during that time. I'll ask my brother, see if he knows."

"I have had a little success in canning, but I don't have many recipes. Mom and Tammy really don't can, but I do enjoy it. If some of her recipes are available that would be great!"

"I'll ask around and see if I can find out anything. Well, I have better be going. Got to work early! See you tomorrow alright?"

"Oh yes, sure, I've kept you up late talking. I'll see you tomorrow, I'll make dinner alright?"

"Sounds fine to me. See you about seven?"

Chapter 20

The warm sunny spring day was perfect for planting the garden, as they tilled, raked, and worked the ground smooth together—peas, carrots cucumbers, beans, corn, squash, strawberries, and tomatoes. She could imagine eating a juicy ripe tomato, as in melted in her mouth, exploding in flavor. Tomatoes had always been her favorite, even as a child. The warm April sun bathed her soul, infusing her with earthy delight. Basking in its warmth, she paused and thought for a moment. *I can't wait for fresh garden vegetables.... I need to plant chives, parsley, garlic, basil and rosemary too! I'm really glad Matt likes to garden also... I wonder if he likes caned jams, fruits and vegetables. There is just something about spring that is so fresh and new. Working in the dirt is just so invigorating!* The rich dark earth felt good in her hands, soft and cool to the touch. She enjoyed the feel of the soil surrounding her skin, she would never use gardening gloves. Enjoying the smell of the dirt, she savored it's rich deep scent, as it filled her senses, spurring her to continue planting. Taking another deep breath, she exhaled, enjoying the spring day.

"Hey, daydreamer! I have planted two rows of corn while you haven't even finished planting one tomato yet." Matt teased her.

"Sorry, I was just enjoying the outdoors," she explained as she finished packing the dirt carefully around the first tomato. Sandi started planting the next tomato. Lilacs in full bloom mixing with the fragrant roses and forsythia filled the air with a rich mixture of perfume. Tiny little johnny jump-ups dotted her front lawn. Well, it wasn't much of a lawn really, more a mix of weeds and wild flowers she mowed every week.

That afternoon with the garden planted, Sandi and Matt decided to go to the veterinary clinic and check on a horse that had been brought in yesterday. The owner was moving out of state and unable to take the animal with them.

"I'm glad they found a job, but sad for the horse. I just want to make sure he's doing okay. We're not set up for horses really, so I had to come up with a makeshift corral. It is too small for him though. I'm thinking of enclosing part of my barn and make a yard for him at my house, so he will be a little more comfortable. What would we need to do that?" she asked.

"Hmmm," Matt thought out loud, "You already have a nice barnyard area, just reinforce the fence. The barn is in good condition, but you will need a water and food trough, and hay for the floor. Just section off what you will want for the horse. Let's see, so… fencing, three inch nails, wood, two buckets for water and two latches for the fence and stall doors and two or three trash cans with lids for oats and whatnot and you will want a storage shelf. "We could probably get most of this done this weekend." Matt answered thoughtfully. "Do you want to get started right now?"

Working together side by side felt just right, as they tackled the project.

Chapter 21

Later that spring, the snow had all but gone, except in the high country. May was the month of graduations. School was almost out for the summer—just another week. Matt was still frustrated with the lack of progress in the cases. The more answers that seemed to make sense, the more questions arose. It seemed like a never ending cycle. But now that summer vacation was about to begin, he knew he would be busy keeping an eye on bored kids, and there would be little time for solving the cases.

I remember I could hardly wait to get out of school, and when I was out, I was bored to tears! School is one of those blessings in disguise, You hate it but at least you are not bored! I don't know which is worse; school and homework or nothing and boredom. 'Course my Mom and Dad could always find work for me to help out around the house! A few of the high school kids have paper routes or mowing jobs, but still they have too much free time on their hands, and invariably get in trouble or one kind or another. Maybe that is just a sign of maturity, to be bored and yet not get in trouble, but find a constructive way of occupying one's time. Matt thought.

Chapter 22

With the warmer weather the vegetables were exploding with growth! The corn was already a foot tall, and the zucchini were in a race to gain as much foothold in the garden as possible. *Maybe I did not plant them far enough away from the rest of the garden! I'll have to remember that for next summer's garden.* Sandi thought as she surveyed the squash.

Pulling a few pesky weeds, she thought, *these weeds sure took off too! I can't even keep up! I do believe the zucchini and weeds are in a high speed race to crowd out the rest of the vegetables!*

Sandi had hired two high school girls to help at the veterinary clinic, with Doc Spencer leaving at the end of the month; she needed more help to keep up with cleaning and feeding at the clinic. Each of the girls seemed to be genuinely interested in working, not in sitting around talking to each other all day. *I would not abide that. I pay them to work not chat!* One of Sandi's employees, Julia lived down the street from her, and came over often to help with Diego, Sandi's equestrian house guest, or…barn guest rather. Diego was feeling spunky, as he pranced around his stall, nickering. The horse was watching her, hoping for a ride. "All right Diego, We'll go for a ride" she reached up and patted the horse, stroking his neck.

Getting into the saddle, Sandi led him thru the orchard, and into the forest land that butted up against her property at the back. Matching the horses' rhythm she was enjoying the wind in her hair as Diego broke into a gallop, the stresses of the day began falling away with each stride.

Looking around as she rode, Sandi marveled at spring's beauty, so different from fall, with all of autumns' deep rich burgundies and reds. Spring was full of soft yellows, delicate pinks and mellow blues. The pocked, white bark of the paper birch was beautiful against the blue green of the Colorado blue spruce and Norfolk pines. Sleepy aspen awaking from winter's slumber sprang forth with bright green leaves. Little penstamon stood tall and proud, dotting the forest floor and elegant columbine in blues and pinks graced the shadiest of areas. Low growing juniper clung to the ground as it crept along covering rocks and earth alike as a living carpet. Mossy lichen clung to scrub oak still bare of foliage creating a lacy canopy.

Sandi often found riding thru the country side peaceful, calming her spirit and clearing her mind. *Lord, Thank You for this horse, he is such a blessing to me. Thanks for all your blessings in my life. Give me wisdom with Matt. Thank you for creating such beauty in each season.*

Stopping at the lake, she dismounted and sat down on a large rock, letting the horse drink. Watching a little brown lizard sun himself on a nearby rock, she soaked up the warmth of the sun. Diego nibbled at tender, sweet, young grass. Magpies screeched in nearby trees. Chattering birds and the deep vibrato of the bull frogs heralded the arrival of warm weather. Honking geese flying overhead added to the symphony of nature. *I just love the sight and sounds of nature. That's one of the reasons I bought the house, not like the toxic chaotic atmosphere of San Francisco. I do not miss the smog or noise at all.* Fifty yards from where she sat, Sandi could hear some of the local teenagers' splashing in the lake, enjoying the benefits of the hot summer day. *Boy, sometimes I wish I was still a kid, carefree with no responsibilities.* Chuckling she watched as one of the boys cannonballed off the dam into the lake, splashing water all over a group of delighted giggling girls who had been flirting, trying to get their attention.

Diego nickered as he nudged her, wanting to run again, "Okay, but I have got to head back, boy,

I have a lot of things to do today. I'll see if Julia can ride you later on."

Mounting up, she rode past the dam, heading home. The kids she had been watching from a distance, yelling about a rifle caught her attention. Looking towards the dam, one of the boys, soaking wet was holding up something. *Kids what they do to impress their girlfriends! Probably just a stick!* Chuckling to herself, she urged the horse home.

Chapter 23

The double doors of the police station burst open as a group of teenagers entered interrupting the busy hum of the station. Mike Bradford rose to control the noisy, chaotic disruption. *Summertime and bored kids.* He sighed. "All right, quiet down,… quiet down, what is so important that you kids came in here?"

Instant confusion ensued as all of the teenagers launched into individual explanations of why they were there. "Quiet down… quiet down…one at a time now." Mike sighed "Ryan White, why don't you tell me what happened."

"I found a rifle" Ryan explained as he held up the object.

"Okay. I'll need to take that into custody." Officer Bradford stated as he took the rifle, noticing the safety was off, Mike felt instant alarm and quickly engaged it. "Where did you kids find this rifle?"

"In the lake," Ryan answered. "We were swimming and I dove in and found it laying on the bottom!"

"Okay, sit right down here Ryan and let me fill out this report," Mike stated as he put an identification tag on the rifle. The weapon had defiantly been in the water. Taking out a blank report form He started filling it out by hand.

"Alright… You found the rifle in the water… On the river side or up in the lake?"

"In the lake…in the water…or I mean under the water. I was under the water when I found the rifle……… on the bottom." the boy answered.

"Alright. In the lake…… and let's see…. Are you the only one who touched it today?" Mike wished he could write faster, he would type it later. He struggled with the new technology…*Ugg ……computers*. He was a good officer, just not a computer genus.

"Yes sir!"

"Has anyone else touched the rifle besides you?"

"No sir."

"Did you take the safety off and try to fire the weapon?"

"No." Ryan answered bewildered at the question.

"Are you sure?"

"Yes."

'Benson felt a growing uneasiness as he advised the teens "Alright kids, the dam and river are going to be off limits until this investigation is over, Might be a few weeks, so you will need to find something else to do this summer."

"Aww man, it's hot and we go up there to cool off." the group of teenagers protested.

"Sorry kids, it will be off limits pending further investigation."

"What!? We didn't do anything wrong," they protested in unison.

"No, you didn't do anything wrong, but we need to do our jobs. The dam, and river, that whole area is off limits. You can find something else to occupy your time this summer. I don't want to have to contact parents."

"Man, I told you not to tell the police, Ryan. Now it's all your fault we can't go up there," a tall lanky blonde lad whined as he blamed Ryan.

"It is not Ryan's fault, He did what was right. The dam area is off limits. Do you all understand? Am I going to have problems with any of you? " Mike asked sternly, looking directly at the blonde lad.

Grumbling, the teenagers nodded in unwilling agreement as they left.

Mike looked the Smith and Wesson rifle over, again checking that the safety was on, *This has been in the water quite a while,* he noted as he took the gun down to ballistics.

Sitting back at his desk, Mike radioed Matt just before leaving "10 Adam 4"

"This is 4, what's up?"

"Matt? Meet me at the dam.   A few of the local teens brought in a weapon, said they found it there"

"Will do, 10-4, out"

Chapter 24

Doc Spencer's last day at the office was one of tearful good byes and well-wishing as he hugged his furry clients. He loved each pet as a family member. Sandi told him he could come by each day to visit. *I don't know what else to say, I feel so bad. I wish he did not have to retire. I knew this day was coming, but well, I just...I guess I thought things would stay the way they are. Why does life have to be so unfair sometimes?* Even the cookies and punch she had brought didn't help her feel any better about his forced retirement. *If only it wasn't for health reasons. If it could have been 'cause He wanted to.*

Thankful the emotional day was finally over. *A quiet evening is just what I need.* Stopping at the grocery store, she picked up some meat, hamburger buns, pickles and chips. *Maybe some chocolate chip cookies would be nice, I really like Toll House Cookies I'll need some chocolate chips and brown sugar for that.* Leaving with her groceries she headed home.

Getting out her measuring cups and mixing bowl, Sandi prepared to bake, as she gathered the rest of the ingredients she would need for cookies. Her mouth watered in anticipation of the chocolaty delights and her stomach agreed.

Chapter 25

The two officers waited on the top of the dam for the diver to surface, their police dogs by their sides. The heavily treed area was so different than when Mike had been injured last winter. Gone were the heavy winter snows. Aspens tall, and stately, now stood at attention in full foliage next to graceful evergreens. Beautiful Paper Birch swayed next to them, in the light breeze. Blackberry bushes in full bloom mixed with wild lilacs created a savory sweet perfume. Still using his cane, Officer Mike Bradford painfully recalled sliding thru those Blackberry brambles when he broke his ankle last winter and shuttered just thinking about it, remembering that terrible thorny decent.

"Mike, I didn't see anything down by the river head when I checked," Matt informed him.

"The kids said they found the weapon in the lake"

"True, and I have called a diver in, to dive down in the lake, but I was checking the river side, just a hunch I'm working on."

"Anything you want to share?"

"Not yet, I'm not even sure it makes sense."

"Ahh, I understand those hunches, the diver has come up. Let's go check with him," Mike said as he nodded in agreement. Walking along the top of the dam's structure only eighteen inches wide, the officers could see where the kids had been goofing off earlier. "Someone left behind one tennis shoe, Chapstick®, and a white t-shirt. I found some flip flips down below by the mouth of the river." noted Matt informing his partner.

Will, a slim man, surfaced and sat down on a large rock, taking off his diving mask and fins.

"Well?" Matt asked expectantly.

"Not much to tell. I didn't see anything worth reporting, just rocks, mud and debris. And a muddy shoe. Do you want me to retrieve it for you?"

"What size?"

"Kids shoe maybe a 5 or 6" Will answered.

"Want me to retrieve the shoe?" he asked again.

"No, we don't need the shoe. Thanks." Both officers walked back to their waiting patrol cars, to finish filling out their documentation.

Chapter 26

"Hi Sandi" Matt greeted her as he came in from work. "Must have been a hard day. You are baking cookies. Mmmm, smells like chocolate chip! My favorite!"

"Yes, I didn't think today would be so hard, but it was emotionally draining to watch Dr. Spencer retire. I didn't think it would affect me so. I knew he was going to retire when he hired me last winter, but somehow, I just thought something would work out and he would not have to leave"

"I understand. I think we are all sad to see Doc. retire." Coming up from behind, he gently put his arms around her. "You have flour in your hair!"

"How was your day?" as she asked as she relaxed into his embrace.

"Good! We may have finally had a break in one of the cases! That would be fantastic. I am so ready to have these solved and get on with it. Hmmm......Looks like fixings for hamburgers too." He commented.

"Yes, I guess I was in the mood for comfort food tonight," She smiled.

"Comfort food is good. I'll do the meat then start the grill. Okay? Let me wash my hands first."

"Yeah, Thanks. I guess I got involved with the cookies."

"They sure smell good!" Matt observed as he inhaled the aroma in delight. "I always enjoy eating homemade cookies."

Outside on the wraparound porch, Matt started the grill, then placing the meat on, seared the hamburger to perfection. In no time they were sitting down to dinner, enjoying the warm summer evening. Sparrows excitingly chattering away were constructing a nest in one of the trees nearby.

Bringing out a plate of freshly baked Toll House cookies after dinner, they enjoyed the warm treat as they sat on the porch swing that Matt had hung last week. "This swing was a good idea, Matt! I wasn't sure at first, but now I'm really glad you put it up."

"My folks had one and I really enjoyed it when I was a kid." He reminisced. "Spent many an hour reading on that swing. I like the two blue flower pots full of pink petunias you put on either side of the front door. They sure enhance the entrance.

Makes it more welcoming," Matt noted sounding a little distant.

"You seem quiet tonight, anything wrong?" Sandi asked.

"No, I was just thinking the job, trying to work things out in my mind. I shouldn't bring work home."

"Can I help with anything? Sometimes it helps to have a listening ear."

"No, just thinking things through, not even sure if any of it makes sense. Listen, I have to work early in the morning, so I'm going to head home and get some rest. I'll see you tomorrow, alright?"

"Okay, see you tomorrow."

"Good Night."

"Good Night." Smiling Sandi leaned against the front door frame *I have a good life here! This was a good move here!*

………

Gunshots rang out piercing the night. Julia awoke, jerked from a sound sleep, unsure of what it was. Dread filled her heart. Slipping into her bathrobe, she found her parents in the family's living room, worried. Her father was loading his rifle, their German Sheppard was growling at the front door.

"Mom, Dad, what was that?"

"I'm not sure, but I'm going outside to take a look around, keep the dog inside. Lock all the doors after me. Honey, call the police," Julia's dad instructed as he opened the door. Angry voices could be heard yelling above their dog's incessant barking. A woman screamed as another shot rang out.

"Sounds like the new vet's place! Call 911!" her dad shouted over his shoulder as he raced towards the noise. Even though Ben was a large man, he ran swiftly down the street, grateful his loved ones were safe at home behind locked doors. *What is going on? It's escalating! Faster! I need to run faster!* He could hear the agitated horse shrill scream in his stall. A man was loudly yelling. A woman kept yelling "No!".... Another gun shot rang out!...... Dogs barking at the noisy altercation......

I need to run faster!... He stumbled in the yard, dropping his rifle...... *Where is it? Maybe I should forget the weapon and just run to help...No I'd probably get shot myself...... Where is my rifle?* Crawling on his knees, sifting thru the grass, frustrated at the time it was taking to find the gun...... searching in the darkness for his weapon, he felt impending doom; he almost left it ... *Where is my rifle?......there it is.* He felt a smooth round cylinder, picking it up, he yanked hard. It didn't budge. Feeling along the cold smoothness, he felt the base of a tree as the root joined into the trunk. *Just a tree root......blast it all! Where is my rifle......* A flashlight shone.

"Ben? Do you hear this? What is going on? What are you doing?"

"I tripped and lost my rifle!" Ben cried in desperation.

The neighbor shone his flashlight around the area. A gleam shone as the light rested upon the cold sterile metal of the barrel. "There!" … …Another gunshot rang out "Come on!" he urged in desperation.

Grabbing the rifle the two men sprinted toward the angry voices. Approaching the house they could see Sandi on the front porch in her bathrobe, only one slipper on, having lost the other. The gunman brandishing his weapon in one hand as he dragged her toward his car. She was putting up a fight yelling "No, Stop it. My home is here." The horse who had been distraught by the conflict, was strangely quiet in his stall now. Sandi's six month old pup joined in the angry fray, grabbing ahold of the assailant's pant leg, trying to be ferocious, only to be kicked aside.

"You are coming with me!" The gunman yelled dragging Sandi towards his car.

She struggled against him grabbing hold of the banister. "No, my life is here."

"Your life is with me, and I'll tell you where we are going to live! You will do as I say, you ungrateful slut!"

"I am not going with…you," she yelled.

"You will do as I say. You promised to love and obey Me!" He yelled.

"Get in the car! You tramp!"

"No!" Still struggling to gain her independence.

"Get in the car, slut! Get in!" dragging her closer to her transportation to prison. "Get in!"

"No! My life is here! Leave me alone! Stop it! Stop it! Let me go!"

"You will do as I say! Get in the car, you tramp! Get in," he demanded angrily, overpowering her as he dragged her closer to his car. "Get in the car!"

The argument kept getting louder and louder, as the perpetrator dragged her off the porch toward his red convertible, so out of place in the rural town. Sandi, kicking and screaming, fought every step of the way as he inched her closer and closer to the prison he offered her. He had the advantage with shoes on. She, barefoot now, was unable to mount a strong defense in the loose gravel on her driveway, having lost both of her slippers in the fight.

Ben could see a few more of his fellow neighbors hiding behind tree trunks with guns in hand. He heard the sirens approaching, closer and closer.

"I've got an idea. Let's block his car so he can't escape." His neighbor hissed.

"How, stand in front of it? Not me!"

106

"Rocks! Cover me," was the whispered reply.

"Rocks?" Ben, unable to fathom the answer, watched as the neighbor set his weapon down, picked up a good sized rock, crept over to the car jamming it in front of the tire. Unable to find a second rock, he proceeded to let air out of the tire.

"Let go of me!" Sandi demanded still struggling against her assailant.

"You are coming home with me where you belong!"

"Let go of me! Stop it! Let go!"

Two police units flooded the yard in the next instant. "This is the Harmony Falls Police. Stop what you are doing and put your hands up!" boomed the authoritative voice thru the megaphone.

"Don't come any closer or I'll shoot her!" The gunman yelled still struggling to control her.

"Let the hostage go, and we'll talk," the officer demanded.

"No, she's not a hostage. She's coming with me," He yelled.

"I am not going with you," she angrily cried as she tried to gain her freedom from his grasp.

"Let her go," the officer advised.

"She is coming with me! This is none of your concern." The brute yelled still struggling to control Sandi, brandishing the weapon in his left hand.

"I am not going with you!" Sandi emphatically cried still struggling against the man.

"Get in the car!" He demanded. "Get in you slut!"

"Let the hostage go!" the policeman sternly warned.

Ben watched as the gunman inched closer to his vehicle dragging Sandi, *What are the police waiting for? Just shoot him! Shoot the jerk!*

Another patrol car pulled in the crowded yard, Bradford grabbed his rifle as he got out of his car, horrified at what he was witnessing. His canine officer Max, leaped over the back of the seat pushing past him, almost knocking Matt down in his determination to protect.

"Let the woman go," The officer again demanded over the megaphone.

"No, she is mine!"

Bradford joined up with the rest of the force behind one of the cars. "Bradford, do you know anything about this guy?"

Matt's mind flashed to the flowers and card he had found in the trash and wished he had read that card, it all started to make sense why she had been so distant towards him when he first met her. His mind racing he thought, *Who could this guy be?*

Sandi's brother in law, Officer Bill Brown, crept up and answered the question on everyone's mind. "This is Sandi's ex. They divorced because he was abusive. Name is Todd—Ray Todd. She moved here to get away from him. A real nut job."

Matt's massive German Sheppard saw his moment and sprang forward. The trained canine grabbed the gunman by the throat, careful not to break the skin, knocking Sandi and her assailant down, in the process—the gun fired. Every one automatically ducked hoping to not be the target of a stray bullet.

"Get him off me; He's going to kill me. Get him off!" the man screamed, feeling the canines' hot breath on his throat. "Get him off! Get him off! Get him off!"

In the darkness the chaos that ensued was hard to follow as to what happened in the next instant. The police swarmed in seizing the gun, handcuffing the man. With the big dog standing guard, the gunman was too terrified to move as he stared into the barred fangs of the massive well-trained dog. Muscles tensed, a deep throaty growl kept any thought of escaping at bay.

Matt raced over to Sandi placing his arms protectively around her, tenderly and carefully helping her up onto the porch, and into the house. Sitting on the sofa, he waited a few minutes as she started hysterically crying, releasing the tension of the night, shivering. Matt pulled the afghan off the back of the sofa and wrapped it around her.

"Want to tell me happened? Who is this man?" So full of questions, he felt like those questions would explode out of his chest as he waited impatiently for her to answer. Irritated that she not only did not tell him before this, but she withheld vital information. Vital, not only to protect her, but the neighbors in this rural community, the children that lived and played in the community, those that he considered his family in this town. Irritated that she did not trust him enough with this information. He would have understood. It was his job to protect her, didn't she realize that? *It is my job to protect not just her, but others as well! Maybe we are not as close as I thought.* Waiting for the crying to subside, Matt's thoughts raced trying to put into place all the pieces to the puzzle, his emotions churning. *I respect her privacy, but people could have been seriously hurt, or worse, and what about us? Does she not trust me? Does she not feel the same closeness to me as I feel for her?*

Bill Brown came in and walked over to his sister in law, concern in his eyes "Sandi, honey, Tammy is on the phone, she's concerned. She wants to talk to you."

Taking the phone, Sandi sobbed into the receiver "Hi Tammy......I'm okay... ...No......No......I can't live my whole life with you or Mom and Dad...... Okay, I'll consider it...... Okay......bye" Sandi shoulders slumped in discouragement, "I can't believe he tracked me here" she sobbed "I thought he would leave me alone! I didn't tell anyone I was moving here, just you guys and Mom and Dad." She sobbed.

"Talk to me Sandi, Who is this guy? Why won't he leave you alone? I want to help you" Matt urged her. "I can't help you if you don't talk to me."

Sniffling Sandi started to relay a few details of her previous life. "I married right out of college. He seemed wonderful while we were dating. But as soon as we were married, he quit his job, expecting me to support him. He was so jealous. Wouldn't even allow me to talk to my family. After the divorce, I stayed with my folks for a year, it was a nasty divorce. It was so bad I couldn't even stay in my apartment, he harassed even my neighbors, eventually the apartment manager asked me to leave because of the constant bullying. When I was at my folk's place, he still would come over and stalk me, whether it was at work or going home, constantly following me, daily… even parking outside the house all night. If by chance I went to Arby's, he would know exactly what I ate, who I had lunch with, how many times I refilled my soda, what I drank whether it was Pepsi or Coke or ice tea. I got a restraining order but the police were so busy that each time I called them to enforce it, somehow he knew just when to leave before they arrived. I had a few dates after that but each time he would follow them and intimidate them. One time he almost ran one date down with his van. His vehicle was just inches away from my date. I felt I needed to move out of San Francisco, before someone got hurt or killed, and my folks agreed.

I'm sorry I didn't tell you Matt, I thought moving here solved the problem. Tammy thought it was a good idea to move here too and Bill would be around to keep me safe. But then a few months ago I started getting letters or a card and flowers. I didn't think he would go so far as to come to Harmony Falls and try to drag me back. I thought he would leave me alone after I left. You have no idea how bad it really was living with him."

"Is that what the flowers and card were in the trash?"

She gasped "How do you…?"

"I was throwing weeds into the trash," he answered her question. "Sandi when you have a problem, I want to know about it. I want to be a part of your life. I consider us an item. I can't do that if you don't confide in me."

Weeping softly again, tears coursing down her cheeks she whispered, "I'm so sorry Matt. I thought it had all ended."

Overcome with compassion Matt put his arms around her again, "It's okay love. I'm sorry I was so harsh, this incident could have been much worse. I just want to be a part of your life, and I want you be a part of mine."

Cradling her in his arms, Matt looked up to see his brother Mike Bradford had entered the room, head down, his hat in his hand.

"Uh…huh." Clearing his throat at this time "Matt …umm… there is something you need to know about outside."

Matt got up and left Sandi with Officer Brown, following Mike to the barn where Matt could see a group of men standing around in the dark. "Mike what is so important that we have to come all the way out here?"

"Just go look," Mike instructed nodding towards the barn.

Entering the large structure, He went into the stall, and looked down at the horse, struggling for its last breath. "A stray bullet hit the horse in the chest, he won't last long. Do you want to tell Sandi now? Or is the shock……?"

Matt thought for a second, watching the life ebb out of the horse, "No, I better break it to her now.

Chapter 27

With heavy heart Matt went back inside the house, dreading what he must tell her *Lord, help me tell her. Give her strength to go through this."* He wished he could take her place right now. He wished he could take away the pain of her former life, the divorce. Blast it! It seemed so unfair to suffer so much just 'cause someone else it a big fat jerk! Taking a deep breath, He approached, "Sandi, umm…its Diego."

"What about Diego?"

"He's been injured." Matt wished from the bottom of his heart he didn't have to tell her this, but it was the best way. "You had better come."

Sandi flew out the door, racing toward the corral, ignoring the fact she was barefoot, she felt no pain running on the rocky driveway. Pushing past the men, she knelt down in the dirt by the horse, who whinnied softly at her. Crying, she noticed the blood gushing from the gunshot wound and knew it would not be long. There was nothing she could do as a veterinarian. "Diego...... Oh Diego, I'm so sorry," as the horse breathed it last. Weeping over the death of her beloved animal, she cried till she could cry no more. She wished she could have prevented all this. "It's all my fault...Oh Diego, I am so sorry."

One by one each of the men quietly slipped away as she knelt there mourning the loss of her horse. The first streaks of predawn light touched the night. Each neighbor left, feeling bad for the beautiful veterinarian and her horse, thankful their families were safe, realizing the ugliness in the world had touched their lives and their quiet peaceful town—ugliness that police everywhere dealt with daily.

Even though the officers had taken the vermin away an hour ago, the filth of his actions had touched their tranquil lives forever.

Matt gently helped Sandi up and escorted her back into the house. Crying from exhaustion, she finally fell asleep on the sofa during those early morning hours. Covering her up with the afghan thrown off earlier, Matt went outside to think, about the murder, the theft, this—was it all connected or just coincidence? *How could each incident be tied in with the next? Just a rouse? A distraction so he could kidnap Sandi right under their noses, while they dealt with another situation?*

Matt looked up when Officer Brown came outside. "She loves you, you know. She just made a mistake by not confiding in you about this."

"I know. I'm thinking about everything that has been going on in Harmony Falls and about that also. I think if I were in her shoes, I would probably do the same, hoping he would leave me alone. Unfortunately, abusive individuals do not think like the rest of us. I'm going to take a few days off, and spend some time with her. Partly for safety, partly for her sanity, and partly for my sake! I'll be back on Monday. I need to figure a few things out."

"I understand. I would feel better with you around here," Brown agreed.

"Why don't you go on home to your wife? She is expecting, I wouldn't want this to cause problems. Since I'm staying here for a few days, would you pick up a few things for me?" Matt asked.

"Better yet pal, go home and pack a few things, I'll stay here until you get back. Alright?"

"Okay, be right back." Matt agreed getting in his patrol car; he drove home.

Chapter 28

Sandi slept until late Monday afternoon. Sitting up she noticed Matt was asleep in the easy chair across from her, Max and Toby sleeping at his feet.

Quietly rising she went into the bathroom to begin her day. Wakened by her movements, Max watched her. Glancing out the bathroom window, something about the sun seemed odd, she couldn't place why at the moment, it just seemed to be too low. As she began to get ready for work she started remembering the events of the night before. She sighed, "I wonder if I'll ever be rid of him?" Going outside she made her way to Diego's stall now empty. Sitting on a bale of hay, she started weeping again, feeling the heavy emptiness that deep sorrow brings—the all-consuming grief that comes with loss.

Going back into the house, she put the hot water on for tea, not hearing Matt come up behind her. She jumped up when he put his arms around her.

"Take it easy" Matt said gently as he guided her to a chair; he sat down in the chair next to her.

"I'm sorry Matt. I guess I have messed everything up and now Diego is gone. It's all my fault..." her voice trailed off as she began to wept.

"Shhh, it's not your fault, at all. The man is sick. It is his fault. It is his illness. Don't blame yourself. Sometimes life is not fair. You mustn't blame yourself. Don't take responsibility for something that is not yours. If you do that, it only enables them to continue being sick. They'll never get help that way. Listen, I know this is hard, but we'll get thru this...together, alright?" Matt gently admonished her. "I'll let you freshen up, then we'll go out to dinner."

"Okay, I'll change." Calming down, she went to change.

While she was upstairs, Matt freshened up in the downstairs bath, after feeding both of the dogs he let them outside for a few minutes.

"What time is it anyway? You said we'll go out to dinner, not breakfast." Sandi stood in the doorway, waiting for his answer.

"You slept until after four o'clock."

"That late?" She gasped as the realization of the hour set in.

"Yes, you had a hard day yesterday. It's allowed. I also took the liberty of having Bill put a closed sign on the clinic for a few days."

Chapter 29

Yawning, Matt and his canine, Max walked into the station and started the coffee. He never could stand the powdered stuff, so searching thru the refrigerator for the creamer but, not finding it, he'd have to settle. *Seems like everyone else likes the good stuff too! I'll have to get some at the grocery store this weekend.*

Walking thru the darkened station, He turned on the lights, and sat down at his desk. *The only real good thing about working at this time of the morning is the fact everyone in town is asleep still. So...I can catch up on paperwork and finish my coffee!*

Sipping the piping hot drink, Matt leaned back and put his feet up on his desk relaxing for a minute. There were times when he had fallen asleep during these early shifts, but the coffee was taking effect, clearing his mind. He thought about the search up at the dam yesterday. Except for the rifle, all of the other items found, seemed to be things the kids left behind in their excitement. He knew the ballistics report on the weapon the kids found, would not be ready until later on this afternoon at best. Matt still had a feeling in his gut … *something…Just wish I could put my finger on it.* Taking out both files he set the photos in separate piles and started reading.

Thirty minutes later the phone rang … first call of the day … *maybe it's just a lost kitten and I could finish…*

"Police, This is Officer Matt Bradford. Hmmm … alright ………… Okay ……okay……Be right there"

Hanging up, He grabbed his hat and looked at Max "Well boy, it seems like the day has started already, let's go."

Driving out to the location, the summer day was already hot; Matt left the window down so Max would be more comfortable.

Grabbing his notepad, He walked up to the accident "Hi folks. Mind telling me what happened here?"

"I pulled out from Starbucks drinking my coffee and ran into Bill. I didn't look where I was going. Spilled my coffee down my trousers"

Looking down Matt noticed the coffee stain then turning his attention to the man standing next to him asked, "Is that the way you see it Bill?"

"Yes. Accidents happen."

"Alright, I'll take a few measurements and file my report. You'll be able to pick up a copy this afternoon."

After gathering the information he needed, Matt headed back toward the station, but first he stopped at the jewelry store.

"Morning Matt, I have the item ready for you. When are you going to ask her?" the store clerk greeted him.

"Well, not sure. It has to be the right ambiance, you know, and our schedules aren't always the same."

"I can well imagine, you being an officer and all. I don't suppose you could put out an all-points bulletin, just tell everyone you'll be busy for several hours to ask your girl," the clerk handed him a small velvet box. "So what do you think?" waiting for the officer's smile of approval.

Taking out the ring, "Yes, I think she'll like this," He said as he carefully inspected the ring's beauty, enchanted by the brilliance of the stone. Smiling, he felt good about his choice. Placing the ring back in the box, He asked, "What do I owe you?"

"Do you want that on credit or cash?"

"I'll do credit."

Paying for the ring, Matt got back in his patrol car and drove back to the station, smiling as he imagined Sandi's excited, "Yes", to his question of lifetime bliss.

Grabbing a cup of coffee and a donut, Matt sat down at his desk to fill out his report. But, first he took the ring out of the box it was nestled in and admired the beauty of the craftsmanship. Placing the ring back in its case, he locked the treasure safely in the top drawer of his desk.

Better not lose this in a day's work! Sandi would kill me if that happened. Now just plan the perfect moment to ask her! Could borrow a horse and go riding, or a picnic, or a really nice dinner, or some guys hire a plane to write, "Will you marry me?" in smoke in the sky. So many options, How about a hot air balloon ride? Pop the question holding a big bouquet of flowers tied with the ring and ribbons? Bowling? So far I like the idea of hiking the best. She enjoys riding. No, that would just remind her of Diego. I could hide it in the garden, she could just happen to find it. No, that would come across like a mistake; no lady would like to be treated so casually. No, a picnic sounds like the best idea! I know of a sweet little cave up by the waterfall. It's a longer hike, but the view is worth the trip.

Chapter 30

Officer Matt Bradford called his brother late that night "Mike, I've been working on a hunch. Meet me in the profile room tomorrow morning with the files and ballistics reports. Okay?"

Picking up the required ballistics reports the next morning, Officer Mike waited for his fellow officer in the room, wondering what Matt had been working on. *What was this hunch? He had mentioned one several days ago.*

Matt arrived with coffee in hand, opening the documents they started to work thru the details. It seemed routine enough. Both of the weapons were 30-06 Smith and Wesson hunting rifles, but that is where the similarities ended. Both look identical except for the butt of each weapon,

Examining the ballistic report pictures, Matt closely examined the photos of each weapon's striation, knurls, and ejector markings.

Hmmm......... "I got a magnifying glass in my desk. I'll be right back."

Rising he went into the other room and pulled out the magnifying glass out of the top drawer of his desk. Returning to the profile room he studied each photo closely again. *Hmmm......Hmmm...... un huh......Hmmm...... Yes that's it......Yes, I'm sure of it...*

"Will you tell me what you are thinking instead of humming everything," Mike commented exasperated.

"Yes, I guess that would be irritating. Well, these are my thoughts." Handing the magnifying glass to his fellow officer, Matt started to explain.

"See the striation marks? They match here and here. Also on the coroners' report has the same mark, but not in the photos from the robbery. Notice the knurls—they are the same in these two photos and the same with the ejector markings, these two are the same, but, this photo from the robbery is different."

Mike Bradford carefully examined each photo "Yes. Yes, I see that!"

Officer Matt went on, "I believe the rifle that was found in the lake was the one that killed Mr. Wills. It is also the one he was hunting with. He went hunting alone in the high country when he sighted a deer, took aim, releasing the safety. Then, decided to get a clearer shot, crossed over the icy surface of the dam, slipped on the ice, the gun fired, Mr. Wills was injured in the chest. The weapon landed in the lake, and Raymond Wills fell down by the river head. With no one to go for help, he bled out and died. This is when you found him. The weapon Mr. Wills was hunting with is the one that killed him.

"The weapon stolen from the Millers' home was pawned in a shop for cash. Just a robbery." Bradford surmised as he explained the theory.

"I agree with you. It makes a lot of sense."

"Yes, Mr. Will's death was just an accident and not a homicide. The robbery was just that—a robbery."

Chapter 31

Planning the perfect proposal was hard work. It had to be perfect, down to the finest detail, especially for the most beautiful woman in the world. Matt's mind was not on the weeds he was pulling in the garden. No, it was on orchestrating the perfect plan.

Yesterday they had driven into the big city for dinner, then a walk at a local park, talking about recent events, Sandi's ex, staying safe, dreams, their goals, but more importantly, a future—their future—together. Matt felt a change in their relationship—a new, and deeper, commitment, and in turn, Sandi felt much more comfortable fully trusting this man standing beside her, who was willing to love and protect her. Sandi relayed in great length the details of her previous marriage to Ray Todd. Uninterrupted, they had been able to work thru the issues that had hindered their relationship before. Together they worked thru issues, building a solid foundation for their lives together—one built on trust and openness.

Grabbing another handful of weeds, Matt pulled them up in one swift yank, his mind still on the breakthrough in their commitment to each other, that fact brought warmth to his heart. *It is truly amazing and fantastic how it makes you feel—to know that someone loves you! Companionship is a many splendid thing!*

"I don't know where you mind is today, but you just pulled up a bean plant!" Sandi's laughter rang out. "Are you okay? Or is there something I need to know?"

Her laughter was good to hear again, like music to his ears, after all they had been through. "Mmm, sorry, I guess my mind is elsewhere. Think the bean plant will survive or shall I just let it go?"

"Well, I doubt it will produce anything by the end of summer, let it go, besides, I think we'll have enough beans. You want to tell me what's going on?"

"Not yet, I'll tell you later." Matt smiled; he just almost spilled the proverbial beans. He wished from the bottom of his heart the perfect moment had arrived, but he would have to wait and finish preparing.

That big moment would arrive soon...............

Very soon..............

IF YOU FIND YOURSELF IN AN ABUSIVE RELATIONSHIP;

This author encourages you to check with your local crisis center, police station or talk with your physician; No one needs to live with disrespect or violent behavior. No one needs to tolerate an abusive partner. Cruelty is never okay.

How do you know you are in an abusive relationship? Ask yourself a few questions:

1. Are you treated with respect, especially around others or does he put you down?
2. Does someone break your dishes or tear you clothes up? Does he destroy your things?
3. Does he claim YOU deserve to be treated like this?
4. Does he claim his anger is entirely your fault?
5. Does he call you names like stupid, idiot, or worse?
6. Does he hit, apologize, then a week later hit you again, only to apologize again, only to hit you again, and again repeating the cycle of mistreatment, promising to change?
7. Does he threaten or intimidate you with dangerous objects?
8. Does he tell you that you are worthless?
9. Do you feel obligated to forgive the abuse? (Proverbs. 22:24 NKJV) "Make no

friendship with an angry man; and with a furious man do not go: otherwise you'll learn his ways and get a snare in your soul"
10. Is he irrationally jealous, even if you talk to your sister?

Abuse can be physical, mental, verbal and/or emotional. Remember: IT IS NOT YOUR FAULT! The cycle will only continue and escalate. Please seek help. Only you can break the victim cycle!

OTHER BOOKS TO READ ON THIS SUBJECT;

Untangle
By Terri Savelle Foy

Beauty for Ashes
By Joyce Meyers

Shuugh, God and Lulu
By Lois Fowler Barrett

The Shack
By Wm.Paul Young

Letting Go of Disappointment and
Painful Losses
By Pam Vredevelt

Avoiding Mr. Wrong (and what to do if
you didn't)
By Stephen Arterburn & Dr. Meg J.
Rinck

About the Author

A survivor herself, Marii now lives in the pacific northwest in southern Oregon, surrounded by majestic snowcapped mountains and farmland rich with heritage, with her wonderful husband Norman. She enjoys traveling, writing, gardening, and spending time with her two cats and six grandchildren. In preparation for this series, she has researched the life stories of others who like herself, have survived and escaped abusive situations. After retiring, she turned her passion for writing into publishing books for you to enjoy. The antics of her kitten has inspired the book The Grey Kitten's Forever Home. If you have enjoyed this and other books by this author please write:

TMN/Wisdom Merchants
P.O. Box 481
Klamath Falls, Oregon 97601

OTHER BOOKS BY THIS AUTHOR:

......

Harmony Falls Book 2
It's just a hole punch
(soon to be released)

......

The Grey Kitten's Forever Home

......

The Flower Power Story

www.ingramcontent.com/pod-product-compliance
Lightning Source LLC
Chambersburg PA
CBHW070335130626
46556CB00007B/2879

* 9 7 8 0 9 8 9 4 7 3 5 1 4 *